DESPERATE
SISTERS

Also by Stephanie Johnson

She's Got Issues

Rockin' Robin

Married to the Badge

DESPERATE SISTERS

Stephanie Johnson

www.urbanbooks.net

Urban Books
1199 Straight Path
West Babylon, NY 11704

ISBN-13: 978-1-60162-041-5
ISBN-10: 1-60162-041-1

First Mass Market Printing March 2008
Printed in the United States of America

10 9 8 7 6 5 4 3 2 1

This is a work of fiction. Any references or similarities to actual events, real people, living, or dead, or to real locales are intended to give the novel a sense of reality. Any similarity in other names, characters, places, and incidents is entirely coincidental.

Submit Wholesale Orders to:
Kensington Publishing Corp.
C/O Penguin Group (USA) Inc.
Attention: Order Processing
405 Murray Hill Parkway
East Rutherford, NJ 07073-2316
Phone: 1-800-526-0275
Fax: 1-800-227-9604

Acknowledgments

I'd like to thank my family for their unconditional support. My Mom, sister Kyria, brother Ren, Lyndon Sr., John, DJ and Lyndon, Alexis. I love you so much. No matter what happens, know that I do what I do for you!!!

To the Flava's, namely Ke-Ke Deeks, Zina, Adrienne, Jack-in-the-box, Kim and the newest member Tony, you guys are the best. Thank you so much for listening to my blues. . . . To others who I talk to daily, share my deepest secrets, hurts, tears and cries with, I thank you for your shoulder. You know who you are. And that includes you Tyson, Mommy loves you.

Tysha and Tyshell of Lockame Designs on the West Coast, thank you so much for your support. I'll be out to see you soon. Liz Marro, you are my girl. I love you like a sister. Haze, thanks so much for our friendship. It will always mean the world to me.

To my brother Lorenzo, I'm so proud that you are doing so well. Keep it up and know that I have your back.

And to all my readers, thank you so much for your continued support. Any of you can reach me

ACKNOWLEDGMENTS

at sf07740@yahoo.com or
safjohnson@verizon.net.

Sincerely,

Stephanie

Chapter 1

Jalisa

I didn't know why I did it to myself. I imagined waxing my eyebrows was as painful as giving birth. Not that I had any children, but from what I understood, that mess was no joke. And you would think they would try and get all the hairs with the wax, but no. As soon as they were done stripping your face, they wanted to pull out the tweezers to get the stragglers. Sometimes I wanted to bop Wey Lin in the head.

Normally it wasn't busy at lunchtime on Friday's, but on that particular day the shop was buzzing with women trying to get right for the weekend. Unfortunately, I didn't have any plans for the weekend, so I was okay with sitting my butt there and waiting another half an hour just to be tortured and to get right for myself.

I was hungry as hell, and I needed to get some gas if I planned on making it back to the office.

"Excuse me," I said as I walked over to one of the girls; "how long before someone can wax my eyebrows?"

"One minute more. One minute." Working that file on her customer's fake nails, she spoke through a paper face mask without looking up.

I walked back to where I was sitting and picked up a magazine with Damon Dash's *Ultimate Hustler* advertisement on it—sixteen people were going to compete to become the *Ultimate Hustler.* They'd spend weeks with people they didn't know, only to be in either a bar hall brawl or end up in bed with one of their counterparts. *Nice!* It sounded like fun, but I didn't think I could do it. I was too private and not into letting too many people penetrate my personal space.

"Otay, Miss Jalisa." Wey Lin motioned with her hand for me to follow her.

I tossed the magazine and went into a little room in the back.

She pulled the white paper over the table for me to lay down. She put the wooden stick in the hot wax and slowly slid it below one of my eyebrows. Then she tore off a piece of fabric and lay it on top of the wax, lightly pressing it down. Without warning, she ripped it off.

This was the same routine every time I came, but I was never ready.

A few moments later, she did the other one, then came the tweezers.

I asked, "Why can't you get everything on the first go-round?"

She ignored me and continued plucking the little hairs that she missed.

I broke out in a sweat and felt my eyes welling with tears.

"All done. Pay at the counter. See you two weeks."

I looked in the mirror to see her work. As usual, she hooked me up. I tossed her three dollars and went to the counter to pay. As I was walking out of the shop, in walked this caramel-dipped, triple scoop of something which had me all twisted in the little bells that hung from the door. I gently swatted at them to get a better look as he walked up to the counter.

"How you, Quinton?" Wey Lin was much friendlier with him than she was with me; she had a huge grin on her face. "You want your brows today?" she hummed in her "me love you long time" voice.

"Yes, Wey. The usual." He sat down.

When he answered, I thought the gods were coming down upon me. His baritone voice went through me, all up in my joints, and stopped at the crease of my thighs.

As soon as his firm buttocks hit the chair, she walked over to him, took him by the hand, and led him into the back room.

I was sure I looked stupid standing there. One of the bells was softly jingling. I grabbed it with my loose hand. He didn't notice me staring at him as if I'd never seen a man before. For sure, I did, but not as fine as him anyway. I wished Lyda and Valen were here—they were my best friends. Lyda would know how to handle approaching him.

Umph, umph, umph, it ought to be a sin to look that good. I began to walk out, but I really wanted to make my presence known to Mr. Quinton, at the very least. I hovered along the outside of the shop as I thought about how I could play it off and act like I had some other business in the plaza. "Ah, Wey Lin," I said prancing right back into the shop, "I think you missed a hair or two."

She poked her head out of the back room, where she was taking care of Mr. Quinton. "Okay, okay. Be right there. Have seat."

I sat back down in the same chair that I'd sat in before and waited.

Five minutes later, Mr. Quinton came out. His eyebrows were thick and beautiful. I stared at him as he came around the counter to pay Wey Lin.

"Thank you, Mr. Quinton. I come get ice-cream later."

"Thanks, Wey Lin. And I'll have it made for you in five minutes."

Ice-cream?

He turned around, and we made eye contact. "How are you?" he asked as he walked past me and towards the door.

"Hot. Good, but hot." It was fall already, but telling him that I was hot would explain me going in to get some ice-cream.

"Well, maybe you should come down to the shop and get some ice-cream. It's two doors down on the right."

Bingo. "I think I will. Wey Lin just has to clean me up." I pointed to my brows.

"You look cool to me. Get it?—*cool.*"

Ooookaaay. "Give me five minutes. Go make Wey Lin's sundae thingy and be ready to make mine."

"I'll be waiting." With that, he walked out of the shop.

"What you want now?" Wey Lin came up to me and started poking at my eyebrows. "You eyes look fine."

"They do? Oh, I thought I saw a stray hair when I looked in my rearview mirror."

"Ya, right, Jalisa. You see Quinton and you like." She smiled and her eyes disappeared.

I couldn't help bursting out with laughter. She was really funny-looking. "Okay, Wey Lin, I think you're right, my eyes are fine. I'll see you in two weeks."

"Bye, Jalisa. Tell Quinton I ready for ice-cream."

I gave her two thumbs up as I walked out the door, my stomach in knots. I was never this bold; it was out of character for me. I wasn't spontaneous and didn't really just open up to people. But Mr. Quinton had me thinking about stepping out my comfort zone. Dude had me excited.

I took my time as I walked down to the ice-cream shop because I had no idea what I was going to say to this complete stranger when I reached his place.

When I got there, Quinton was waiting behind the counter wearing a stark white apron and a funny-looking hat. I laughed to myself as I walked around a chair in the middle of the floor and up to the counter.

"Would it be okay if I recommend a special cup of ice-cream for you?"

"Sure. Are you the only one who works here?"

"No. The others are on their lunch break."

"Have a seat, Miss." Quinton directed me to the empty chair. He was putting his game down, as they say.

I sat down. " '*Miss*'? Oh well, you wouldn't know my name because I didn't tell you, *Mister*. It's—"

"I don't need to know your name right now." He opened the ice-cream case and placed two large scoops into a glass goblet."

"That's a big glass."

"Aren't you the least bit spontaneous?"

No. Greedy, but definitely not spontaneous. "Sure, I am." I didn't want him to know that he was reeling me in with his suaveness.

He ignored me and moved over to the counter-top where all the toppings were. With his back to me, I watched him move with quickness while he made my ice-cream sundae.

A few moments later, Quinton turned and faced me. In his hands was this huge goblet of ice-cream. It was so heavy, he had to hold it with two hands. He came from around the counter and stood right in front of me.

I looked up into the bottom of the glass that held what appeared to be butter pecan ice-cream smothered with caramel, fudge, walnuts, pineapples, strawberries, and marshmallows. I knew damn well that I didn't need to eat that, but hell if I was going to turn this sweetness away. "Oh my goodness."

"Yes. You called?" He got on one knee and pulled a spoon from his back pocket.

I reached for the spoon, but he playfully pulled it back.

"Allow me."

I sat there and watched him spoon out ice-cream and a pile of sweet toppings.

He slowly raised it to my mouth, which was already opened, and proceeded to put it in. It was too much, and some of it oozed out of the corners of my mouth. He laughed. "Is it too much for you?"

I shook my head no as I tried to chew and swallow, but ended up just swallowing.

"Ready?" He had another spoonful waiting.

This time I opened my mouth as wide as I could. He guided the spoon into my mouth.

Just when I thought he had it all the way in, I closed my mouth around the spoon. As I ate the ice-cream sundae, a string of caramel dripped onto the side of my cheek.

Without hesitation, Quinton took his finger and gently wiped it off. He looked me in my eyes and put his finger in his mouth. "So what did you think?" he asked, licking the caramel off his finger. He had no qualms about letting me know that he thought I was "sweet."

"It was okay." I tried to hide the fact that he just blew my mind. Not just with this huge, delicious sundae, but also with his confidence and smoothness. "Can I have that to go please?" I had to get out of there before he had all of the toppings out and on me.

"Why the rush?"

"I really need to get back to work. I'm already late, and you know how it is sometimes."

"Well, aren't you going to pay for this sundae?"

"Excuse me?" *I knew this was too good to be true.* I began to reach into my purse as my attitude took over. "Here's your damn—"

"Your phone number would suffice."

Charming chump. I wrote down my phone number as Quinton put my sundae in a container. "Thanks for the sweets."

"There's more where that came from." He took my hand and kissed it.

I left the ice-cream shop with the realization that, in a matter of minutes, a complete stranger got me addicted to his sweets.

Quinton called me a few days later. We began talking on the phone a few times a week. Friday became my eyebrow and ice-cream day. Every time, he made me something different and just as sweet as the first sundae. I felt like I was in heaven. Quinton was everything that any woman would want in a man. He would open doors for me and he sent me flowers a few times. One time he even sent me a fruit bouquet of cantaloupes, melons, strawberries, grapes, and pineapples beautifully arranged in the form of a flower bouquet.

We spent time together once or twice during the week. Maybe a drink after he got off work and I was done with all of my appointments. But the time we spent in the ice-cream shop on Fridays was the best. It was our time, special, flirtatious, and just plain romantic. I looked forward to Fridays because I knew he would have something special for me.

My hours were flexible. I made suit shirts and suits for a living. Basically, I was a glorified seamstress. Business was slow for me in the beginning, and that's why I was able to spend time with him either on the phone or in person. When business picked up on my end, I had less time but always made our Friday date.

His hours, on the other hand, weren't as open as mine. He owned and operated the ice-cream shop and had a few employees. But none of them was one hundred percent dependable, so if someone called out, he had to cover.

We both agreed that we needed "personal space." So instead of spending every night at each other's house, he spent one night over at my house in Neptune, and I spent one at his house in Belmar. This arrangement worked great for us, but then we felt like even that wasn't enough. So we changed it to two nights each at the other's house and still kept our date on Fridays.

Everything was going so good for us. Our time spent together wasn't about anything or anybody but us. Sometimes we'd crawl up on the couch and watch DVD's; other times we'd just sit and talk about stuff in general.

I felt a deep connection with Quinton; he accepted me for who I was and never complained if he was at my house and one of my appointments ran late or whatever. And I, too, understood when he had to close the shop because of lack of help. It seemed like we were on the same page.

And sexually, wow! Quinton made me shiver. The way he touched me when we made love told me that he loved me. And when he said it, oh my gosh! I knew he would love me forever. Our love-making was seductive and playful at the same time. He would bring the whipped cream and cherries home from work, spread the cream on my breasts, top my nipples with a cherry and lick them until they were clean. I would get caramel topping, squeeze it all over his dick, and suck it until he made his own cream. I loved it. Then he would let me ride him. He knew I loved that too, especially facing away from him. Watching him watch my ass bounce up and down made us buck each other until we came together. The way he handled my body turned me on, and the way he talked dirty turned me out.

Quinton and I got really close. The time we spent together was beginning to not be enough. We tried to compensate by talking on the phone more, but again, our schedules didn't allow for that. So after much consideration, we decided to move in together, renting a condo in Red Bank, so that neither of us would feel awkward about sharing our own personal space.

Our schedules continued to be crazy, especially when Quinton closed the ice-cream shop and took on an even bigger endeavor. He'd started classes on owning and operating a restaurant. Upon completion of the course, he opened one of his own. I was really happy for him.

Meanwhile my clients doubled. I got calls from people from the West Coast and thought that it would be a good idea to have someone out there who could do alterations for things that I'd made here. With that in mind, I took out an ad with the help of my friends, Tysha and Tyshel, who were designers and lived in L.A. Within a few weeks, I flew out there to conduct interviews. There were so many applications, mostly from Mexicans or Spanish-speaking women, that I couldn't make my decision right then and there. So I flew back home and reviewed the applications when I had the time.

Nine months into our relationship, Quinton asked me to marry him. After we'd been married for a year, things changed drastically. There was no warning period or trickling off of the affection. Quinton just stopped everything. He no longer teased me with sweets or felt it necessary to be intimate with me. And when we did have sex, it seemed as if I was forcing him to make love to me.

We stopped talking like we used to. The most time we spent together was in the morning when I would be eating and he'd be having coffee and reading the newspaper. I couldn't help feeling like I was losing my marriage, and couldn't figure out, for the life of me, what went wrong.

One day I had enough and confronted Quinton. He wasn't too pleased. "Jalisa, please . . . you sound like a horny sixteen-year-old."

"Excuse me? And you sound like a grumpy old man. What's wrong with your dick all of a sudden? Why aren't you interested in being with me? I'm twenty-six years old and too young for this shit."

"Why are you bothering me with this? You know I'm busy."

"Busy doing what, Quinton? You've had the same schedule for months now, so that has nothing to do with it."

"I think you're making something out of nothing, Jalisa. Maybe you should look into some medicine to calm you down. You've been tripping on this problem you say we have for a minute."

"Forget you, Quinton. I don't have to deal with this. Do you really think I'm beat like that where I don't deserve better? I may have been single for a long time before you, but desperate no, I don't think so. I know what I'm worth, and I'm going to get mine."

A few days later when I was calm, I went through the applications and narrowed it down to two possible women. I made appointments with them and flew back out to California. I used the restaurant in the hotel that I stayed at as the meeting place. The first woman, Maria, was a younger woman. She was a mother of two and claimed she really needed the job, but the entire time I was trying to interview her, her cell phone kept ringing.

"Excuse me," she said for the fifth time. She carried on a conversation for ten minutes about nothing.

I politely interrupted her. "Maria, we're done here."

"Hold on," she said to the person on the telephone. "So I got the job?"

"No, I don't think this is going to work out."

"Tsk! Nobody wants this lame-ass shit anyway. Peace out." She got up and left.

A few minutes later, a woman walked up to where I sat.

I looked up and was taken aback by her beauty.

"Are you Jalisa?" she asked.

"Yes. And you must be Lisette." I stood up and shook her hand. It was soft. "Please, have a seat."

"Thank you. I'm impressed that you would fly way back out here just to interview," Lisette commented.

Dressed in a terry cloth jumpsuit, her eyes were bright, and her hair was pulled back into a ponytail.

"Well, I need to make sure that the person who will be working with me is a perfect fit. People are funny about their clothes, especially when they pay the amount of money they do to have them custom-made and tailored."

"I understand. So where should we start?"

Lisette and I went over her experience as a seamstress. At the time she worked in a men's clothing store making small alterations. Then she elaborated on her talents, pulling out pictures of dresses that she'd made for weddings and christenings.

"Wow! You are very good."

"Thank you. Back home, that's all the women did was sew."

" 'Back home'? Where is back home?"

"Brazil."

"Interesting." I looked at her mouth as she spoke about her family there. As she sat across from me, her arms were folded in front of her, and her breasts rested on them, pushing them up and giving her very nice cleavage.

"You know, Lisette, I think this will be a good time to offer you the job."

"Really? Oh, thank you." She jumped up and came over to me.

I got up, and she gave me a hug. The warmth of her body turned me on. "Would you like to come up to my room for a drink, you know, to celebrate our new partnership?"

"Yes, I'd love to."

We went upstairs, ordered two bottles of wine, and before I knew it, I was sprawled out on the bed with Lisette's head between my legs.

Chapter 2

Jalisa

It was 10:30 and he was asleep already. His back to me, Quinton snored like a wild pig. I was completely turned off by his grunts and growls.

I was especially heated with how the evening went. I'd planned all day for an evening of "hot, erotic lumps on my forehead by the end of the night" sex. I cleaned all morning. I baked the cake that would go into my classic strawberry shortcake truffle and made homemade whipped cream. Then I went to the food store to get dinner. When I came back, I put the food away, cut up fresh strawberries and the cake. I got my truffle bowl out and layered it with cake, strawberries, and whipped cream, twice, then tossed it in the refrigerator.

I went upstairs, turned on my XM radio, and listened to some music while I rummaged through my many pieces of lingerie to find the perfect one.

I liked to walk around in sexy little get-ups. It made me horny.

I changed into something I'd made especially for Quinton. "Ah, this should do it," I said as I picked a pink, frosted, sheer camisole with matching crotchless panties. I lay it on the bed then drew a hot bath. While the tub was filling, I placed a few drops of jasmine vanilla oil into it. "I love this stuff."

I took off my clothes, shaved my legs, underarms, and my precious spot then lowered myself into the hot, steamy bath. The water seductively moved over my entire body, forcing me to drop deeper into the tub, leaving only my head above the water. As I allowed the hot water to completely relax my loins, I opened my legs so that my lips were parted. I slowly reached down in between my legs. By now my clit was swollen from the hot water. I softly touched it. I thought about how I wanted to tie Quinton onto the bed, straddle him, and ride him until the cows came home. I imagined his toes curled, then spread, curled then spread, as I put my hips into mad motion on his magic stick. With these thoughts, I quickened the flicker on my clit and softly pinched my nipple with my free hand. I was aroused by my touches and thought about how Lisette licked my pussy when I was in California.

That day when I interviewed her, we went up to my hotel room where we waited for wine to be brought up and had idle chitchat. I was so attracted to her. I shocked myself at the thoughts I had of her. The wine came shortly thereafter. We had one glass, then another. I moved toward her, and she accepted my lips as I kissed her. As we kissed, we undressed each other and went to work. She licked me from my pussy to my ass. I had my legs wide open and held her head there so that she could get to taste it all. I returned the favor and tasted her too. She was bitter, but I enjoyed her flavor. I'd never been with a woman before, but would do it again if I knew it would be as good as it was with her.

I continued my private party until I had an orgasm. After my body stopped quivering I got out of the bath, dried off, put on some jasmine vanilla lotion, and put on my little outfit. I laughed to myself because my little friend between my legs was still excited. Guess she wasn't done. "Momma's got you, don't worry." I fluffed my hair, put on my robe, and put on the finishing touches for the evening with Tina Marie playing in the background.

I placed tiered pillar candles in every room and lined the hallway to our bedroom with tea lights. In the bedroom there were two trays of food: one with two lobsters, asparagus, and wild rice, and the other with my strawberry truffle. I placed rose petals on the new satin sheets I'd bought and opened the windows with the hopes that the evening air would blow some serious sex voodoo my way. I also turned the phones off.

When Quinton came home, I met him at the door with three huge white feathers, two lay across and covered my oversized, erect nipples, and one hid my most precious pearl. I had a glass of champagne in each hand. My hair was tight, and my body was glistening with shimmering body lotion. I thought I'd succeeded in setting the mood. Oh, how I was mistaken!

The minute he walked in the door he started with his mess. "I'm so tired." He threw his brief-case on the couch and removed his suit jacket.

"Let me get that for you, sweetheart." I took his jacket and tossed it onto the floor. I handed him a glass of champagne. He downed it and handed the empty glass back to me.

This is not sexy. I filled it again and handed it back to him. I felt an attitude creeping on, so I took a sip of my champagne and tried to relax as I listened to him. I was trying really hard to be patient and understanding, but I was quickly developing a case of attention deficit disorder.

"I swear those people at that restaurant—"

"Listen, baby, why don't you get undressed, go take a shower, and I'll meet you in the bedroom," I said, rudely interrupting him. I could give a damn about the people at the restaurant. I was horny, the juices were oozing from my pearl, and my lips were swelling more and more by the minute. I needed to get laid, damn it! I had no time for the small talk!

I followed him as he walked up the stairs and tipped back his glass of champagne two or three more times. He stepped out of his shoes and left them right outside the bedroom door. I stepped over them and into the bedroom, closing the door behind me. I sat my glass down and walked over to the stereo. I turned it up a little bit so that Tina could serenade us into a state of sexual euphoria. *WRONG!*

"Can you turn that music down, please. And be sure you blow out the candles; they can cause a fire. I have a serious headache. And what are you wearing? You look ridiculous."

Oh no, he didn't. I picked up my glass. " 'Ridiculous,' Quinton? 'Ridiculous'? Fuck you, Quinton."

"All this is nice, but you know, I'm tired. And feathers? Not my thing."

"No, I don't know. When did you become such an ass? You are such an insensitive bastard."

"I'm tired, Jalisa, and am not in the mood for your theatrics." He sat at the end of the bed and took off his socks.

I threw back the rest of my drink. Most of it dripped down out of my mouth and onto my feathers that covered my now deflated nipples. *Tired? Theatrics?* "Quinton O'Neil, it's been two weeks since we've made love or had any physical contact with each other. I can't even get a hug or a kiss when you walk through the door from a 'tiresome and hectic' day. I'm saying, what's the problem? When do you plan on fucking me?"

"Jalisa, quit it already." He took me by my shoulders, that pissed me off, and began to tug at the silk strings that held my damp feather get-up together.

I got them loose and let the feathers fall to the floor. I walked over to the closet, grabbed my kimono robe, and put it on.

"Jalisa, maybe we could do this some other time."

"No, Quinton, I'm tired of your rejections. If it's

not one thing, it's another. You never want to have sex or be intimate with me. I don't understand how someone who so-called love sex and loved to be with me when we first got together can just cut it off just like that." I snapped my fingers and put my hands on my hips.

"I still got it; I'm just not in the mood to give it up."

"What? I know you're not serious. Quinton, we've only been married for almost a year now and we've had sex all of ten times. Maybe ten and a half, if you want to count the time you came as soon as you put it in."

He glared at me.

"Well, you did."

"When, Jalisa? You're always trying to play somebody out."

"That time when we were having phone sex. Remember, you were downstairs, and I was upstairs. You were talking about how you would take my legs and spread them."

"Yeah, I remember now."

I knew he didn't want me to finish. "Well, you should, because that was it. By the time I came downstairs, you were ready to cum, and as soon as I sat on it, that's exactly what your tired ass did."

"We were talking dirty for ten minutes already, Jalisa. What did you expect me to do?"

"How about make love to me?"

"Jalisa, the honeymoon is over."

The honeymoon is over. This joker! Valen and Lyda are going to love this.

"Let me tell you something, I need passion; I need to feel you; I need to know that you still desire me. We have no children that we need to put to bed before we get busy, so I'm telling you right now we really need to address this issue."

"I'm tired and I'm going to bed."

So here I lay next to a man who had no interest in making me feel like his wife. Ay, I think I said it in plain English. He heard everything I said. I know he did because I heard it myself. He refused to see the importance of our being intimate by invalidating my feelings. *I'll fix him.*

I turned onto my back. On my nightstand was my XM radio. I put on my headphones and turned to a station that was playing Gerald Levert. I began to move my hips to the music. I massaged my nipple with one hand then slid my other hand in between my legs. I was hot. I was frustrated because I needed this action. All I could think about was him, or some damn body sucking my toes and rubbing my calves. Then I thought about him running his tongue along my thighs. I spread my legs a little bit wider and fantasized about him tasting my overheated love tunnel. He would say the alphabet with his tongue and then he would go in and out as I touched my clit. I moaned for him to go deeper, but he wouldn't or couldn't. Who knew? He needed to move from taking me with his tongue to taking me with his manhood.

As I mentally seduced myself, I managed to turn over onto my side. For a minute I almost forgot Quinton was in the bed; I was so into it, I tuned out his breathing.

"Can you be still?" Quinton mumbled.

"Quinton, you should be doing this." I continued to freak myself right there in the bed while his "no-sex-giving" butt lay right next to me. I pushed myself back and forth as I rode my own three fingers, determined to deliver an orgasm that would leave me more satisfied than Quinton had been leaving me lately.

"Um, yes, take this," I moaned out loud. I was wet, dripping wet, and was getting wetter by the minute at the thought that Quinton didn't know what he was missing and that I was doing myself good. Damn good. "Yes!" I tilted my head back as if my hair was being pulled by my lover and exploded. My body fell limp and onto Quinton.

"Girl, what are you doing?"

"What you can't seem to do. You ain't shit, Quinton."

"You are so selfish, Jalisa. I work all day long, and all I want to do is come home and relax."

"You are an ass, Quinton. You should want to come home to me, but I guess that's changed in the last couple of months." I got out of bed. "This 'no having sex' thing you're trying to have going on is not happening, somebody will take care of me if you don't."

"Well, maybe that's what you need to do."

"Excuse me?"

"You heard me, maybe you need to do you since you need something that I apparently can't give."

"Wait, I want to get this right, are you telling me to get my sexual needs met elsewhere?"

He was quiet.

"Quinton!"

"What I'm saying is that if you need to have somebody to tell you that you're beautiful, make passionate love to you, pay you all sorts of attention, or whatever, then go and do you. Find that man then. We're in two totally different places right now, and you just need to do you if that's what's going to make you happy."

"I'm telling you that I want to be with you, love touching you, and you tell me to go have sex with somebody else? Boy, Quinton, that's a good one. I didn't say anything about needing you to tell me how good I look, I already know that. I'm your wife, and I need you to be a husband, can you do that?"

"Jalisa . . ."

"Guess not. I'm sleeping on the couch. Good night, jackass." I stormed out of the bedroom. I cried as I lay on the couch, feeling rejected and undesirable. *Something's gotta give. Either Quinton steps up his game, or maybe I'll need to book a flight to California to see if Lisette was in the giving mood.* Yes, I think I needed to go see Lisette.

Chapter 3

Jalisa

"I just want to tell you that what you did last night was completely uncalled for," Quinton blurted out.

I knew what I'd done the night before would be the topic of discussion at breakfast. I continued to butter my toast.

"What happened to understanding?"

He just knew how to whine. *Ugh*!

" 'Understanding,' Quinton? I always had to understand you and why you came home every day with a twisted face as if someone pissed in your cornflakes. I always had to understand why you're just too tired to have sex. I'm tired of understanding, and I'm tired of being rejected."

"Wait a minute. I understand when you're on your period and don't want to be bothered. And I don't reject you; I just wasn't in the mood."

"No, Quinton. You understand because, just

like any other night, you're not interested and obviously don't want to be bothered. If you've lost interest in me, aren't attracted to me any more or found something new and exciting, you need to say that, I'm a big girl; I'll be okay. And a husband who loves his wife is always in the mood. Sex isn't always about the physical." I got up and went to the refrigerator to get the orange juice.

The phone rang.

"Jalisa, you know—"

"Hello." I answered the phone with an attitude.

"Ill," Lyda said.

"Yeah, what's wrong with you?" Valen asked.

"Hey, y'all. What's up?"

"Nothing. What are you doing?" Valen asked.

Lyda laughed. "Sounds like she might be fussing with Quinton."

"Yes, you would be right about that."

"Well, call us when you get a chance. What's this argument about? He still ain't giving you any?"

"Bye, fools." I hung up the phone and turned my attention back to Quinton.

"Quinton, I'm too young for this. I'm trying to get it on. I'm horny as hell and I'm tired of masturbating. I'm not saying that you have to tongue me down every time you see me, but damn! Can I get a kiss on the lips? I have never heard of a husband not wanting to kiss his wife on the lips. And to make it so bad I never had to ask you to love me before. It seems like ever since we got married, slowly but surely you removed the passion from our relationship." I was getting emotional, so I just grabbed a glass, poured my orange juice, and sat down. "I need to feel your passion, Quinton."

I ate my breakfast quietly while he continued to justify himself and his "limp Richard."

"I'm sorry if you don't understand that I'm trying to take care of us and make sure that we have money in the bank. Someday you're going to want children and you'll thank me for working all of these hours so that you can stay home with them."

I haven't said a word about having any damn kids. And don't you have to have sex to have children?— idiot!

"I'm doing this for you. I agreed to let you have your little business making suits, travel all over to meet your clients, and do what makes you happy, and this is how you show your appreciation? You're never satisfied with anything I do, so like I said, if what we have isn't good enough, go do you."

There he goes again with this "go do me" business. What husband in their right mind would tell their wife to go and get what they're missing at home, from somebody else? That wasn't normal. Either he was retarded, or he was doing him, which would explain why I wasn't getting any.

"Quinton, are you having an affair?"

"An affair?" He laughed.

"Well, are you?"

"When do I have time to have an affair, Jalisa?"

"In the beginning, you were so passionate, eager to please me sexually, and couldn't keep your hands off of me. But for the last couple of months you've completely shut me down. Let me ask you this, are you gay?"

"No, I'm not gay."

"I'm not happy, Quinton. I really want this marriage to work, but it doesn't seem you're interested." I drank the last of my orange juice and put my dishes in the sink. "I have to go. I have a client meeting me at the office in fifteen minutes. And don't forget that I have an appointment after work and Lyda and Valen are coming over tonight. Oh, and Quinton, I'm tired of trying to get you to want me. I'm done. I'm going to do me so fuck you!" I walked out.

See what Quinton failed to realize was that with what I did for a living, I could get my needs met at any given moment and he would never know. Whenever I went to size clients, I came face-to-face with penises of some of the finest men. They had their underwear on while I was measuring them, but I could still tell what they were working with.

Making suits had many benefits. Besides having all of my expenses paid up front when I traveled, I got to see all types of men. I'd been propositioned, they'd bought me gifts, and the tips always suggested that they wanted me to do more than make their suits. But I always kept Quinton in mind. I think it was about time to change my view on things. Maybe he was right. I should stop nagging him for intimacy and go find me somebody who wanted to give it up, nag-free and no strings attached.

While I was driving I kept playing back in my mind, *Do you. If that's what makes you happy, then do you.* The words flowed so freely from Quinton's mouth. It was as if he'd thought of them many times before and finally got the balls to say them.

And a huge set they must be for him to say that to me not knowing how I would react. He obviously wasn't concerned with my reaction and thought by telling me to do me, I would shut my mouth, back down from him, and leave well enough alone. Well, he was right.

My client was waiting for me when I pulled up to my office, which was located on Broadway, above a bakery. I loved the location because throughout the day, I could smell the different pastries being made. When the owner felt generous, she would send me up a few of her desserts to sample.

Steven Warren was one of my most loyal clients and he was fine as hell. I'd been suiting him for about six months now. He owned a lingerie company based in New York. He always brought me a catalog of what was coming out, and I would place my order for things that I liked. He'd traveled all over the world selling his products. He was in his mid-thirties, married with children, and had lots of money. I liked Steven not only because he was a cool guy, but also because he always paid in cash.

"Hey, Steven, what's going on?" I gave him a handshake and then unlocked the doors to my office.

"Not much, Jalisa. You look and smell lovely as usual."

His little flirtations always made my day. He always commented on how I looked, smelled, my hair, and even noticed when I changed my lipstick; Quinton never noticed when I wore a different color lipstick any more.

"Thanks. How's the family?"

He followed me upstairs. "Great. No complaints."

"Okay. Good. Now what are you needing today?"

"I need a few shirts made, one white, one gray, and one light pink."

I chuckled. " 'Light pink'?"

"Yes. If these young boys out here can get away with it, so can I," he joked.

"All right. Whatever you want. When was the last time we measured you?" I walked around to my desk and booted my computer so I could look at his file. While it was coming up, I offered him something to drink.

"No thanks, sweetheart. I've had my protein drink, so I'm good."

"Okay, here we go, it's been three months since I last measured you. I think we should get new measurements. Take off your coat." I grabbed my measuring tape out from my drawer and walked back from around my desk. "Put your arms up." Steve smelled especially delicious that day. "Oh, what fragrance is that you're wearing?" I lightly touched his neck.

"Vera Wang."

I noticed he was immediately aroused. "Nice choice."

After I took all of his measurements, we talked a little bit.

He took a seat on the couch that sat in front of the window and waited while I wrote up his bill. "So how is business?"

"I, too, can't complain. I've gotten a lot of new clients, some on the West Coast, and I even have someone on call to measure, quote, or do alterations when needed."

"Wow! Jalisa, that's fabulous. And how is Quinton?"

I cringed. "Quinton is . . ." I paused because I wasn't sure if I wanted to put my business out there like that. Then I thought about Quinton's words, *Do you, if that's what makes you happy.* I was still upset about our discussions.

. . . Quinton is not doing what he should be doing."

"Really? How so?" Steve crossed his legs.

Do you. Do you, if that's what makes you happy. I walked over, handed him his bill, and sat next to him. I looked him in the eyes.

"He doesn't seem to find me sexually attractive these days. I go out of my way to create a sexy mood, and he doesn't seem to catch on. He doesn't think that intimacy is needed in our relationship."

"Most men don't . . . especially if they're bringing in the money. They feel that if they provide for you their job is done. It's unfortunate, but a lot of us are like that."

"So what am I supposed to do? Dry out? Grow cobwebs?" I tugged at his ear.

He laughed. "I hardly think that he'll leave you alone for that length of time."

I could tell Steven was feeling me. "Sure as hell feels like it." I fell back into the couch feeling defeated.

Steven put his arm around me.

I looked at him. I wanted him. I needed to be with him. *Do you. Do you.*

"Have you spoken to him about this and explained to him how it makes you feel?" He leaned in towards me.

"Yes, several times." I kissed his lips.

"And his response was?" He licked my lips.

My pussy was getting wet as hell. "He had tons of excuses that I'm growing tired of. I'm a beautiful woman. I have sexual desires that send flutters all throughout my body. I shouldn't have to beg my husband to want to be with me."

Steven stared at me.

I'd never noticed the intensity in his eyes before. I guess that's because we'd never been this close before. His face was flawless. His eyes were light-brown with dark brown circles around them. His eyelashes were full and curled up to and over his eyelids. His nose wasn't the smallest but wasn't exactly a shotgun either. His lips were shaded by a mustache that was thin and had a strand or two of gray in it. And they were smooth, not a crack in sight.

"You know, Jalisa, we've known each other for sometime now." He grabbed my hand. "If there is anything that you need, you can always come to me." He took my hand and put it on his penis.

Lawd, Jesus, let me get some dick today.

"After all, that's what friends are for."

Do you, if that's what's going to make you happy.

I understood exactly what I was hearing from Steven. He was telling me that if I needed to get laid, he'd help me out like that. I mean, the man was gorgeous. But he was married. He had money and probably did this with all the women. And he had children. But then again we were friends and he looked *scrum-deli-licious.* "What are you saying, Steve?" I played the dumb role as I licked his lips back.

"Jalisa, if you need me, I'm here." Steven kissed me and that was it.

My pussy was like, *Bitch, you better get that dick right now.* "Really?"

"I'm here, aren't I? Do you need me?"

Do you, if that's what's going to make you happy.

"Yes, baby. Damn!"

He smiled and took my face into his hands. With his thumb, he gently rubbed my cheeks while his fingers massaged the back of my head. Steven pulled me to him, and our lips touched again. He pulled back to see my eyes, and I gave him the green light. He stood up, took his shirt off, and hung it on the back of the door.

Do you. I got up from the couch. "I don't know, Steve."

"Are you sure you aren't sure?" He took my hand in his and brought it to his lips. He kissed my fingertips.

Oh lawd, where is Lyda and Valen when I need them? "No," I said through heavy breaths.

He moved closer, took me in his arms, and whispered in my ear. "If there is *anything* you need, Jalisa, you be sure to contact me. I'll meet you anytime, anywhere, all you have to do is call."

"My body is calling; I need you to fuck me right now, Steven." I was wet as all hell.

He began to take my clothes off.

I didn't even try to stop him.

As he removed each piece of clothing, he kissed me, licked me, and bit me.

Inside, I was going crazy. Swarms of butterflies were in my stomach, and I was enjoying every minute of it.

"How does that feel?"

"Good."

"You want this dick?"

"Yes."

Steven guided himself inside of me.

I let my head fall back and took all of him with each stroke. His dick was so thick. I leaned up and watched him go in and out of me. I needed what he was giving to me. Quinton had left me feeling undesirable, and Steven was making good on Quinton's bad.

"Damn, you fuckin' the shit out of me."

"Mmm hmm. Any time you want it, Jalisa, you let me know." He pumped and pumped until he felt me cum. He stepped back, put his shirt back on, and reached into his pocket.

I lay on the couch as he pulled out the cash to pay his bill.

"Thanks, Jalisa. I appreciate you and everything you do for me."

"No Steven, thank *you*. Please just lay the cash on my desk."

He stared right at me, and I smiled.

"So how about breakfast?" he asked.

"I already ate but could go for some sweets. The bakery downstairs has a mean *pain au chocolat*, it's like a croissant filled with rich chocolate crème."

"Any crème is my favorite," he teased.

"Well, then let's go," I said as I got dressed and grabbed my purse.

Steven and I sat at a table in the corner of the bakery, taking in the intoxicating smell of the coffee and espresso. We ordered a sampler platter and two lattés with cinnamon sticks.

As we talked more about our situations, I felt myself leaking. His juices were coming out of me. I licked my lips as I felt his warmth in my panties.

We touched as if we had been lovers before that morning. He expressed how he was happy at home with his wife and their children, but that every man needed that little extra, that "side order of something."

"It's not like I don't love my wife; it's just that she and I both agree that no one person can fulfill their mate one hundred percent." He rubbed my hand.

"So you mean to tell me that your wife knows that you, you know, are with other women? Are you with other women?"

"It's not that way. Take what you're going through for instance. You have everything: a nice house; I presume, a lucrative suit business; nice cars; and a husband. One would look at you and say you have everything, but from what you've told me, none of that matters because he's not connecting with you sexually or, more importantly, mentally. Now if you went and met someone with the idea of hooking up with this person in the back of your mind, would you feel guilty? Would you consider this wrong?"

We looked at each other.

"Yes, I mean no. I wouldn't consider it wrong because . . ."

"Because what?" He took a sip of his latté.

"Because no one person can fulfill their mate one hundred percent."

I watched him as he licked the whipped cream

off his lips. He was making me horny all over again.

"That's right. Affairs are a necessary evil. If you're lucky enough to meet someone that you feel is great and delivers that extra 'umph' and they stay around for a while . . . great. As long as everybody is on the same page, what's the problem?"

"Wow! Is that how men think?" I took his hand up to my mouth and kissed it. I visualized our little sex scene.

He nodded yes.

"I see. The last thing I wanted to do was cheat on Quinton, but you know what, he wasn't listening to anything I tried to say to him. Look what we just did. We are so wrong."

"Don't be silly. Everybody cheats, whether it's mental or physical."

I was silent. I thought about Quinton. Maybe that's why he'd been so distant with me. If he was having an affair or getting sexed up by somebody else, he wouldn't have enough for me. He would be distracted if someone else was whispering things in his ear. I knew Quinton—there was no way he could satisfy two women at a time. So if anybody wasn't going to get it, it would be me.

"I hate to admit it, but you're right." I swirled my latté, once again feeling vanquished."

"Hey," he said as he took my chin, "you'll find your way. Trust me." He wiped his mouth, got up, and kissed me on the nose.

I smiled at him.

He peeled a twenty from his money roll and

went up to pay the bill. "Remember, call me if you need anything else."

"Come here." I kissed him on the lips. "I will." I watched him as he walked out the door. I leaned back in my chair and let my head fall back.

Thoughts of Quinton with another woman swarmed in on me like a tribe of wasps. Faces of different women, beautiful women like Halle Berry, Angela Bassett, and others popped in and out, taking turns teasing me about my man possibly being out there. A few weeks ago, that would've killed me inside, but it was a new me.

I ordered another latté and grabbed my checkbook to balance it when my cell phone rang. It was my evening appointment. They needed to come in earlier, if they could, because something came up.

"Sure, I'll see you in a half an hour." I put my checkbook back in my purse, grabbed my coffee, and went back up to my office, where I waited for my next appointment and thought about the next time I could get some of Stephen's dick. I wanted to take him up on his offer. Today, he was in control; the next time I'd be in control.

Chapter 4

Lyda

Lyda called me as I was daydreaming about my morning with Stephen.

"What are you doing?"

"Chillin'. Come by," I told her.

Needless to say, Steven was all I could think about. After talking with him, I had to admit that I never thought about going out and getting laid by another man. I didn't know if I should feel ashamed or not for doing it. I mean, Quinton did tell me to go and do me. And to think that men did this all the time. When I took my vows with Quinton, I meant them, I swear I did, but this feeling of rejection and being undesirable was really too much for me. As I sat there in my living room, I could still smell Stephen. I flipped through the channels as I drank a cup of tea. Quinton was at the restaurant and for once, that was fine by me. I wasn't ready to look at him anyway. I invited Valen and Lyda over because I knew they were chomping at the bit to know why Quinton and I were arguing this morning. And whenever they were around, he knew to keep his distance. He hated getting caught up in the mix of our *conversations*. His ass had a big ol' bull's-eye on it, so I made sure I told him that they were coming by this evening this morning as I walked out of the door.

"Knock, knock," Lyda said as she walked through the front door.

"Hey now. What's happening? Where's Valen?"

"She's coming. Roger needed her to do something first. She should be here in a few minutes."

"That dude is so stiff. He has no personality whatsoever."

"Yeah, well that's her man. I'd take that over the mess I have any day."

"Aw. Is Anthony still coming too quickly?"

"Yes. And, Jalisa, it is not funny. Got any more tea?"

"In the kitchen." I motioned with my head.

Lyda got her tea then came back and sat next to me on the couch. "So."

"So what?"

"Spit it out, why were you and Quinton arguing?"

"The usual. I'm tired of him acting like making love to me is a chore. I do everything I can to make him feel loved and show him that I'm still in love with him, but he refuses to reciprocate."

"He's too young to have those issues, you know." She held her finger up and slowly let it drop.

"I agree. But it's not that. He told me that he still has it but just isn't giving it up."

"What kind of mess is that?" Lyda blew on her tea.

"Girl, hell if I know." I sipped my tea.

I often wondered if my girls were my girls for real. I wanted to tell Lyda about my conversation with Steven, but I didn't know. I mean we were cool and had been for years now. In fact Lyda, Valen, and I were like sisters.

"You think *you* got it bad? Anthony can't last more than three minutes. Look we're doing it, right," Lyda got up, placed her teacup on a nearby table, and started humping the air. "We're riding and all, and the next thing you know, he just stops." She had one leg in the air and was in mid-hump.

"You are a fool." I was dying.

She quickened her hump.

My gut was killing me, I was laughing so hard.

When I finally got it together, I realized that Valen still wasn't there. "Where is that chick?" I reached for the phone.

Lyda walked around the room humping the air.

We both busted out laughing again.

"Shhhh, it's ringing." After five rings, the answering machine came on. "Valen, it's Jalisa and Lyda. We were expecting you. Give me a call. Maybe we'll swing by, pick you up, and grab something to eat. Bye, girl."

"Whew, I'm hungry after all this work I'm putting in." By this time, Lyda was humping my door frame.

"Maybe I need to be doing that."

"Well, you'll be guaranteed a hard one. Hey, have you ever gone on one of those websites where people meet and chat?"

"No, but I imagine that would be a lot of fun."

"It is. Valen goes on every so often to a singles page."

"What? I'm scared of her."

"Yup."

"She'll have to fill me in on this. Let's go grab her and get something to eat."

"Sounds good to me. Get dressed. I'll be outside."

I went upstairs to put on some clothes and met Lyda in the car.

As we pulled up to Valen and Roger's house, we noticed that the only light on in the house was from the computer monitor, which faced the front of the house, and could be seen through a huge bay window with open curtains.

"There's no one in there. Maybe they're in the back doing the nasty," Lyda said.

"Let's go."

We got out of the car and walked up to the house. The sensored porch lights came on. We knocked on the door, but there was no answer.

"Call her from your cell phone," I said to Lyda.

She did. There was still no answer.

I backed up and leaned over to try and get a better look into the house. From where we were, I couldn't. So we walked around the house to their bedroom window as quietly as we could. We could see the glare of the television through the curtains and a body moving around on the bed.

"What are they doing?"

"How do I know? I'm out here with you."

We leaned on the window and saw them in missionary position having sex. We looked for a minute more, wishing we were the ones getting sexed up like she was.

Roger flipped her over and started sexing her doggie-style as he pulled her long hair.

"Get it, girl." Lyda started humping the air.

I laughed as I shushed her up. "Be quiet, girl. Damn!" We continued to watch them do their thing in silence for a few moments. I wasn't mad at her. Somebody needed to be getting it, but hell if I was going to sit out there and watch her husband do her when mine won't even kiss me.

"Okay, look, we know she's home. Let's go and get something to eat. Between you humping the air and her getting humped, I'm jealous and had enough of the both of y'all." I turned to walk away when I realized something—*Valen doesn't have long hair*—I stopped in my tracks. "Lyda."

"What, girl? Can't I watch?"

"Is he still holding onto her hair?"

"Yeah. Why?"

I turned around and went back to the window. Sure enough, he was bucking her from behind and grabbing her hair. "Since when did you know Valen to have long hair?"

We both looked at each other.

"Oh hell no. Call her ass. Get her on the phone right now!"

"Shush," I told Lyda. "We already tried, but I'll try again." I proceeded to dial her cell phone. My hands were shaking. I kept looking into the window to make sure that what I was seeing was for real. I couldn't believe Roger. I knew he was an ass, but this was crazy.

"I'm going to knock on the door."

"No. Let's wait for Valen to get here."

Meanwhile, she still hadn't answered the phone.

"You can wait if you want to. I'm about to bust this window out." Lyda looked on the ground for something to throw through the window.

"No, girl, you can't do that."

"Why not?"

"Just wait. I'm trying to call her; I don't want to get arrested."

"I'm going to knock on the front door then and bust this thing wide open." Lyda began to walk towards the front of the house.

Valen's voicemail picked up. "Valen, girl, call me back ASAP. It's very important." I hung up the phone and followed Lyda to the front of the house.

"Hello, Valen. It's Lyda and Jalisa. You home, girl?" Lyda banged on the door as she shuffled from one foot to the other. "Hello!" She yelled louder and banged harder. "He's got some nerve. He wants to be all 'Mr. Drill Sergeant' with Valen and have some other ho in her bed. I'm getting real pissed off sitting out here." She raised her hand to bang on the door again. "Forget this mess." Lyda backed up a little bit and kicked the door.

"What are you doing? Give him a chance to open the door. You're going to get us arrested. Damn, girl!"

"I could give a high hell. I'm not gonna sit here and let my girl's man get his off with some other chick. Bump that!" She kicked and kicked until she realized she couldn't kick the door open.

"Lyda wait, let's be rational."

She was breathing hard and sweating as well. "'Rational'? If Valen and I walked up on your man having sex with another chick, would you want us to be rational?"

She had a point. I would think that my girls would have my back and step to Quinton. I thought about it for a minute then stood by Lyda's side as we kicked the door until we shattered the side glass panel.

Lyda kicked the glass out so that we could open the door.

Valen's computer monitor gave us a little light in an otherwise dark house. We knew her house, but we'd never had to maneuver around it in pitch black. Lyda led as I held onto her shirt and followed. We took baby steps until we reached the back of the house. The bedroom door was closed.

I moved Lyda to the side and got in the front. "Let me, because I can see where this is going."

"You got ten seconds before I bust through this door. Ten, nine . . ."

I slowly opened the door and stuck my head in. It smelled like latex and funky sex. "P.U." I squinted in an effort to see. It was definitely Roger doing it to somebody, but that somebody definitely wasn't Valen. "Nope, that's not her."

". . . one . . ." Lyda pushed me right through the door. "You are so busted with your punk ass. Jalisa, find the light. Turn on the light."

I was so nervous and scared. Out of all of us, Lyda definitely was the most rambunctious. She damn near attacked Roger.

"Get off! You're supposed to be my girl's man." She pushed Roger off the woman. The woman, however, wasn't screaming or anything. She didn't defend Roger at all. In fact, all she did was lay there.

I finally got the light on and couldn't believe my eyes.

"You have got to be fuckin' kidding me." Lyda began to laugh hysterically.

"Oh my God." I walked closer to the bed.

"What the hell are you two doing in my house? How did you get in here?" Roger was pissed.

"Roger, Roger, Roger . . . it's one thing to cheat, but with this?" I looked at Lyda, who was still laughing to the point where her face was drenched with tears. "You know, as a woman it's one thing to find out that your man is cheating, but to find out that he's cheating with—"

"Wait," Lyda interrupted. "This is great, you know, if you were my man and I found out that this is how you got down, I wouldn't know if I should be angry, or what."

"Get out!"

"Okay, we're out of here. I'm sure Valen will get a kick out of this one. Does she know about her?" Lyda pointed to his sex toy.

"Get the hell out of my house," he yelled as he grabbed the sheets and tried to cover himself and the blow up doll.

"Okay, my brother, we are leaving you and Barbie to finish getting your groove on. If we see Valen, we'll let her know that we checked on you and everything is good."

Lyda continued to laugh.

I didn't think it was funny at all that Valen's husband was doing it to a black Barbie blow up doll. It was life-size and had the exact same features as the little Barbie doll. He had her dressed in a tailored military uniform, a short camouflage skirt, a tight, white button-down shirt that exposed her perky breasts, and a pair of military boots. Not to mention the green hard hat that was laying on the floor. It must've fell off when he was doing her doggie-style. She had long black hair, her eyes were kind of slanted, and she was the color of milk chocolate.

I would've been devastated if I ever found out that my husband chose a blow up doll over me. Valen was going to be crushed when we told her.

"I'm going home. Roger has worn me out," Lyda said as she tried to stop laughing but couldn't. "Take me home, girl, take me home. And did you see what I saw?"

"Lyda, I don't think that's funny. I mean, if Roger is doing this, what is Quinton doing? And yes, I saw Roger doing it to a blow up doll."

"I thought I'd seen everything, but Roger has proved me wrong."

We both became quiet because we knew the next step was to tell Valen about her husband. *How do you tell your friend that her husband was cheating on her with a blow up doll?* If I knew Valen, she was going to be so upset. She loved this jackass, and now we had to tell her how low he stooped.

Chapter 5

Valen

It was the middle of the week. Why Roger had to have these golf clubs today was beyond me. *Couldn't he have waited until Saturday?* Roger knew I hated to travel at night on these dark highways, but he was so anxious to get me out of the house. I didn't see the importance of golf clubs right now. I was in the house in my nightclothes, relaxing.

"Why do you have to have them now? Or better yet, why can't you go get them yourself?"

"I'm teaching Quinton to play golf. I would go and get them, but I have some paperwork to do."

He knew how to manipulate me. If it weren't for Quinton or, should I say, Jalisa, I probably wouldn't have been so cooperative. I didn't let him off that easy though; I pushed a little more. "What did you do all day that you weren't able to get the clubs yourself?"

"Does that matter? Can you get them or not?"

"Roger, I'll go and get them, but when I get back we need to have a talk." I felt in my gut he was up to something. I looked over at him and watched him as he read some paperwork. He never looked up at me the entire time we talked.

"Yeah, okay," he mumbled, his head still down.

I left aggravated. I was forever letting him take advantage of me. Sometimes I got angry with myself because I should be stronger than that. *When I get home, he's going to know just how I feel.*

I was riding down Route 18, and all of a sudden the front end of my car began to shake on the driver's side. I pulled over to the side of the road, and lo and behold, I had a flat tire. "Damn it! Damn him! I told Roger these tires needed to be replaced." For weeks, I'd been afraid that I would get a flat tire in the middle of Timbuktu.

I turned on my cell phone and my voice mail indicator went off. I ignored it and called Roger but got no answer.

I tried to call him five minutes later and still got no answer. It was dark outside, and I wasn't feeling easy about being alone on the road with a flat tire. Since Roger hadn't answered the phone, I had no choice but to call AAA. "Hi, I'm on Route 18 and I have a flat tire. Can you send somebody? And please make it quick."

They told me it would be about ten to fifteen minutes.

Half an hour later, I was still waiting for AAA. I didn't want to be out there all night. *I've never changed a tire before, but how hard can it be? Guess I need to get myself out there and get started.* I tucked my purse under the passenger's seat to be safe. *Never know who or what could be lurking on these dark streets.*

"Ouch!" I was tearing my knuckles up on the lugs. "I wish they would hurry up."

I got as far as getting the tire off and was completely frustrated. Just as I gave up, roadside assistance pulled up.

"Ma'am, let me help you with that," this person said as he ran towards me, turned on his flashlight and aimed it right at my face.

Startled, I got up and moved backwards.

"Sorry I took so long. I had another emergency up the road." He knelt down to take a look at my tire. "So you know how to change a tire a little bit." He stood up and looked at me then turned and walked to his truck.

A few moments later he returned with flares to line the side of the road, and his tools to finish fixing the tire. "Why don't you get in my truck until I'm done?"

"No, thanks. I'm fine here."

"Suit yourself," he said as he finished changing my tire.

I went on the other side of the car and waited as this man who took nearly a half an hour to come, changed my tire in less than five minutes.

"Okay, we're done here." He stood up. "Is there anything else I can do for you?"

"No, thank you. What do I owe you?"

"Nothing."

"Nothing?" I opened the passenger's side door and reached for my wallet and heard the message indicator in my cell phone going off again. I pulled out a twenty and handed it to him.

"I'm insulted."

"Why? It's a tip."

"Thanks, but no thanks. We're not allowed to take tips."

"Well, suit yourself then." I tucked the twenty in my pocket and proceeded to walk around the back of the car to the driver's side.

"I don't bite," he joked as he packed up his tools.

"I didn't mean to."

"I know." He opened the door for her. "Take my card and call me if you ever need roadside assistance again." He reached into his shirt pocket and handed me his business card.

I took it, got in the car and pulled off. All I could think about was the many times I told Roger that I needed my tires changed. He was such an ass. I reached for my phone and listened to the message. Jalisa sounded kind of frantic. I decided to call her when I got home. I needed to get in touch with Roger and give him a piece of my mind. I called the house phone again, and this time he answered.

"You know what, I know you heard the phone ring just a bit ago. I was trying to call you because I was stuck on the side of the road."

"Is that right? Well, maybe we can talk about this later. I'm busy on the computer." He hung up the phone in my ear.

I looked at the phone in shock.

When I got home, Roger was still busy at his

computer. I busted into his office and threw my purse and coat on the chair. "I got a flat tire on the way to get your damn golf clubs and you have the nerve to hang up the phone on me?"

"Um hmm. Is this where you get all excited about nothing? It was a measly flat. You have AAA. Please tell me you had the sense to call them."

"I can't believe you. What did I do to make you have such ill feelings towards me?"

He ignored my question.

I moved closer to him.

"Roger, why didn't you have the tires replaced? I told you several times that they were worn down and I was afraid that this would happen. You seem like you could care less that I'm upset. Can you be more of a bastard?"

"I'll take care of it tomorrow, Valen."

"Forget you, Roger, I'll take care of it myself. I've had it with your funky attitude. You act like I owe you something."

"You are quite ungrateful."

" 'Ungrateful'? Tell me, what do I have to be grateful for? Oh, I should be grateful for this nice house, right?"

"Yes, a lot of women would feel lucky to be in your shoes."

"And I should feel grateful that you give me an allowance every week, that the bills are paid, and that I don't have to worry about anything."

"Yes, that about sums it up." He got up and went over to his bookshelf.

I followed him. I could feel myself getting worked up. I wanted to smack the shit out of him. "So I guess I should be thankful for that thing you put inside of me too. I should be grateful that you come home, pull my panties to the side, and try to stick your penis in me too."

"I've been told that I know how to sock it to 'em."

"Roger, let me tell you something else, your dick is useless. When you're so-called sexing me up, I'm thinking about how many loads of laundry I have to do. When you think you're making me cum, I fake it all the time. I don't even remember the last time I even enjoyed your dick. So you know what, find those women who would love to be in my shoes because I'm about to find me a man that can love me, that appreciates me, and that can fuck the shit out of me, now, muthafucka!" I smacked him and walked away. I could feel his glare on my back. I didn't care; I was fed up.

I couldn't believe we'd come to this. I went in my room and locked the door. I cried as I came to the realization that my marriage was over. I also thought about the beginning of our relationship and that made me even more upset.

Although Roger could be a bastard, he wasn't always like this. When he and I first met, he had just come out of the Army. Roger was five years younger than I was, and at first, my gut feeling told me that our age difference would eventually be an issue. But as most of us do, we didn't listen to our mothers or our gut, and one of them was almost always right.

On our first date, he took me to Arlington Na-

tional Cemetery in Arlington, Virginia and showed
me the Tomb of the Unknown Soldier. He also
showed me the graves of John and Jackie Kennedy,
and the former heavyweight champion, Joe Louis,
who was also a soldier. I was fascinated with his interest in his country and his will to support and
represent it. I thought that demonstrated commitment and felt that if he could commit to complete
strangers, once we got to know each other and entered into a committed relationship, he would be
just as passionate. He also had me train to shoot a
gun. I remember getting so excited; I knew we were
on some Bonnie and Clyde mess then. Since he was
gone a lot, he wanted me to be prepared, just in case.

"Baby, you have to learn how to shoot in case
you have to protect yourself. When word gets around
that a pretty thang like you is home alone, the
fools will be trying to press up and they can't take
no for an answer! You hear me?" was all he said.

I knew he loved me and wanted me safe for
when he returned to me.

After his tour, he enlisted in the Reserves. He
would go away for one week a month and two
weeks during the summer for maneuvers. When
he went away, he would write me a letter the day
before he left and mail it the day that he was sent
out. This was to make sure that I got it the day
after or so. In his letters, he expressed his appreciation for my standing by him while he was away.
His gratitude and undying love was further com-
municated through short poems and stories.

> *In light visions are clear*
> *Darkness holds my soul captive*

And only when I see your face
Can I be freed from darkness

Those few words captured my heart. When Roger came home on his relief, he proposed, and I accepted. Today, those words sounded like bullshit to me.

We had a modest wedding. Both our parents were in attendance. My mother served as my maid of honor, and his father served as his best man. Afterwards, we had a very intimate dinner at a restaurant that was set on the water. I just knew that we'd be in love forever. What a fool I was then, and what a fool I feel like now.

I noticed a change in Roger when he retired from the Reserves. I was sentenced to a life of chilled emotions from him, served on a silver platter. When I tried to ask him what was wrong, he blatantly ignored me as if it were none of my business. I was cut off from any physical contact unless it was on his terms. His terms were simple—if he felt like having sex, we did; if he didn't, we didn't.

Initially, I thought that maybe all this military action had poked holes in his brain and hardened him to the outside world. But Roger wasn't in combat so what could've happened to turn him from a loving husband, saying words that would melt any woman's heart, to a rotten son of a bitch.

We'd been married for three years now. When Roger and I first met, I thought he was shy. It was cute to me when I would talk to him and all he would do was smile a little. He never complained about anything and pretty much let me be me. He always told me that he loved me for my individuality and because I wasn't like the other girls, meaning I tended to him without being asked and never complained when he needed me.

What drew me to Roger was that he protected me. It mattered to him that I felt safe. Though he really was never big on words, the last two years of our marriage seemed like it was a chore for him to be with me.

He never initiated conversation, never asked me what I thought about anything, never asked me to take part in any of the decisions regarding the house or improvements on the house, and insisted on my not bothering him with minor issues like the balding of the tires. All in all, he didn't talk to me unless he needed to ask me something. And even then, it wasn't like he asked me, he told me. The only question he took pride in asking me was whenever we had sex—"Did you come yet?"

The foreplay was all up to me. First of all, I needed to let him know a few days in advance that I wanted to have sex on a certain evening. Wasn't that something? Now, throughout the day of the act, I had to send him notes with descriptive sexual scenarios of us together. I had to send him a dozen roses and a bottle of his favorite champagne. Whatever evening he agreed to grace me with his bone, the show had to be on by six o'clock. That meant that anything that I had to do, like clean, grocery shop, take and pick up his dry cleaning, and shave (he hated hair on me down there) had to be done by then. And if it wasn't, well then I didn't get any at all. He would completely cut me off.

Roger worked hard all day long as a recruiter for the Army and I knew he was stressed out. He wasn't the most pleasant person, but he was my husband nonetheless. His lack of compassion and attentiveness along with his verbal abuse towards me made it evident that he didn't love me like I felt I should be loved.

While I supported him in whatever he did, I felt like our relationship had gotten stale. In an attempt to bring some excitement into our sex life, I tried something new on him one day. I went down on him. It was one of the biggest mistakes of my life. I remember it vividly.

About a year ago, I was out with Lyda shopping for a gift for Jalisa's bachelorette party. We went into this sex shop on Highway 35, and I bought these little pieces of candy that numbed your throat when you ate them. That way you could deep throat your man. I'd never done that before to Roger, or anyone, for that matter, and thought that he would love for me to take him like that; after all, I was his wife.

That evening, I got all dolled up.

He was sitting in the bed reading over enrollment applications when I popped one of those candies, pulled the sheets back, and took him deep into my mouth. I looked him in his eyes as I slid up and down on his shaft and witnessed his reaction go from shocked to complete disgust.

"Where did you get the idea that I wanted you to blow me?"

I stopped mid-slurp. "What?" Ashamed, I got up and put my hand over my mouth.

"What kind of woman do you think I want as my wife?"

"I thought you would enjoy this. I was trying to bring a little spice into our relationship. You've been working so hard, and I wanted you to know that I love you. I love being with you." He made me feel so low.

"Valen, I didn't ask you to do this. I don't want my wife sucking my penis."

The very next day, Roger sat me down and told me, "Only whores go down on men. Blowjobs are for skeezers and young girls who aren't ready for real sex, or high-class call girls or escorts who get paid to do things like that."

Since that day we'd had this regimented sex life. I'd gotten used to the missionary position of sex and his idea of foreplay.

Not only did I have to do all those things to let him know I was in the mood, I also had to address him as "Corporal" Roger and he wasn't even one. I got his need to release down to a science. Every four days, I booked a half an hour with him so that he could get his off and ask his number one question, "Did you come yet?"

I was tired and frustrated. All I wanted was a hot shower and my big king-sized bed. That night wasn't a sex night, so I didn't clean a damn thing. Roger's dry cleaning was still at the dry cleaner's, and as far as food, it was the bare minimum, bread, eggs and milk. If he was hungry, he'd have to fix himself something to eat or go out. It wasn't my concern at that moment.

After my shower, I crawled in my bed and called Jalisa. I missed her call when I was on the side of the road. And speaking of that, Mr. AAA man was all right. Nice guy, and probably had a woman who he made real happy by letting her rub on that baldhead of his. But you know what, I found him attractive and planned on giving him a call to see if he could help me change my tires. I could tell that he found me attractive. *Who knows, maybe he can help me out and give me a little bit of dick.*

Chapter 6

Lyda

I couldn't wait to talk to Valen. Before Jalisa dropped me off, I had her take me to Dunkin' Donuts on Broadway to get a "turbo boost" with an extra shot of espresso for Anthony. I didn't know what was wrong with him, but he couldn't keep it up for even three minutes. Any woman who'd been cut short before would know my pain. But here is how I got in this predicament anyway.

I was at the DMV one day because I had to renew my license. As I was pulling out of the parking lot I saw him. He was sitting in a brand-spanking-new BMW and was looking real chill. I was with Boyfriend at the time. He was working my last nerve, and I took it upon myself to cause a little disturbance. I spun back around and pulled right beside the stranger's car.

* * *

"Ay, why are we back at the DMV?" Boyfriend asked.

I had to think quickly. "I think they misspelled my name on my license." I held up my license, and since his dumb ass couldn't spell for nothing, he didn't know any better.

"Oh yeah, baby, they did."

"Can you take care of it for me?" I batted my eyes and kissed him on his forehead.

Now it was the middle of the afternoon, and DMV was packed. The lines were crazy and I knew it would be at least an hour before he came running out telling me that he couldn't make any changes to my license. *I tell you, I get the dumbest men.* But I didn't need much; all I needed was a man who knew how to work it. He didn't need to know how to spell nothing, he just needed to know how I liked it. And for the record I liked it rough, tough, and long-lasting!

So while Boyfriend went to take care of my business, I put the moves on dude rocking the *B-M-Dub-Yah*!

"Nice ride, cutie pie. What's your name?"

"Thanks. Anthony." He tried to act uninterested.

Hey, wasn't nothing like a challenge to win the stick. "How often do you get to open it up?" I flipped my leg onto my door and tilted my seat back. I wanted him to think I was about to masturbate.

"Damn, baby, not as often as I would like to." He licked his plump lips, which drove me wild.

"So you want to open it?" I let out a moan that was sure to make him rock hard.

"Hell yeah, baby, but I don't think you can handle what swings between these thighs."

"Is that right? What about what's between *these* thighs?" I took my finger and put it in my mouth, like I was sucking my pussy juices off of it. "Try me. The name is Lyda."

I knew damn well that I shouldn't have been playing him out like that in broad daylight, but you know what, I wanted to. I was a freak. I had a Boyfriend and I had boyfriends in addition to him because I just hadn't found one dude that could rock my world and make me not want another. And until I found him, I was gonna play with all the "hard balls."

Anthony got out of his car and walked up to the driver's side of my car.

Mind you, I wasn't really playing with myself. I wanted him to think that so I could see exactly what he was about. He leaned on my door and tried to put his rap down.

"Oh, you wasn't really getting nasty behind this door. Let me find out you're a fake."

"Fake? I think not; I see you're over here."

"So who has the honors of calling you their woman?"

"Not anyone in particular," I told him. He didn't need to know any more than that.

"Who was that with you?"

"Oh, him? That's my friend." I sat up and got out of the car. I stood maybe an inch or two shorter than Anthony.

He was sexy in a nerdy kind of way. His eyes . . . there was something about them that drew me into him. He wore khaki's, a button-down burgundy collared shirt, and a pair of loafers. Penny loafers. I hadn't seen them in I didn't know how long.

What really turned me on was that he was clean-shaven. His eyebrows were waxed, he had a manicure, and I could see the clear polish on his nails.

I looked him up and down and stopped at his crotch. There lay the anaconda of penises. It was almost the length of his inner thigh. I tilted my head to see if I could catch it at a different angle.

Anthony saw me looking. He didn't try to hide it; in fact he casually took his hand and brushed it softly. He was turning me on and he knew it. "How long before you're out of here?"

I thought for a moment. From the looks of Anthony's member, I needed to widen my horizons and see what he was working with. "I'm ready to go now. Follow me."

He got in his car and I got in mine.

Boyfriend was "assed out." We had a good time, but his time was up. He had my license to remember me by.

By the time Anthony and I got to my place, I was so excited. I had hoped that Anthony held the quality of being a good lover. I had plenty of men under my belt and none of them made me scream for mercy. I normally didn't bring a man to my place when I first met them, but I wanted to give Anthony a try at this.

Personally, I thought that women made the mistake of committing to a man too soon. I believed that a girl had to have choices before that one person had you cooking dinner every night, washing his nasty underwear, making sure he had all of his personal hygiene items all of the time, and hopping on one foot because he worked you out like that. Hey, men did it all the time and even when they did settle down, you can best believe they always had a little something on the side. And that's exactly why I wasn't trying to be with one dude.

"Come on in. Can I get you something to drink?" I tossed my purse on the little kitchenette that was tucked in the corner. My place wasn't a five-bedroom home, but it was cute and it was mine. I had a two-bedroom condo, one-and-a-half bath, living room, dining area, eat-in kitchen, my own garage and driveway, and a little patio in the back.

I was chilling, I must say. I wasn't working at the moment because I got laid off a few months earlier, but had saved enough money to get me by for at least a year.

"Yes, thank you that would be great." He smiled and sat on the couch.

"So are you from around here?" I asked him as I bought out a gin and tonic on the rocks. "Here you go."

"Do you have a lime?"

"Sure. I'll be right back." I went into the kitchen, opened the refrigerator, and pulled out a lime. Then I got a knife.

As I tried to turn around, Anthony was right behind me. He took a sip of his drink. We were so close we exchanged breaths. He took the lime and knife from me, moved over to the counter, and began to cut the lime in wedges. Then he moved back over so that he was face-to-face with me again. Anthony was trying to seduce me, and it was working.

He lifted my shirt over my head.

I was really excited at that point. I just met this man, and here we were in my kitchen about to get our freak on. Worked for me.

"Do you mind?" He took another sip of drink with one hand and squeezed the lime on my nipple with the other.

Now you could've already used them to hang your coat on the way Anthony was teasing me, but when he did that, they would've served better as doorknobs.

He took my nipple in his mouth and that was it for me.

"No, I don't mind, as long as you don't." I reached down and felt his penis. *Lawd almighty*! My prayers had been answered. Anthony must've have been nine inches easy. I rubbed and rubbed until I thought I saw smoke.

I took his drink from him and placed it on the counter. I walked forward as he walked backwards. When we got close enough to the couch, I gently pushed him down and unzipped his pants.

My actions told him that today was his lucky day. I pulled his pants down. I could see the imprint of his penis through his Ralph Lauren cotton boxer shorts, the head was sticking out of them. For a minute I was scared. It was big and fat, but it was too late to back down now. *After all, with a piece like this he had to be able to work me out for hours.*

I closed my eyes as I slipped my hand into the opening of his underwear and pulled his penis out. It was hard. Sometimes you get ones that are blotchy or the skin was all crazy, but not his, it was perfect. "It's beautiful."

He laughed then let his head fall back onto the couch when he felt my lips on his manhood. I played with his wand slowly. Slipping up and sliding down his shaft made me wet. I don't think I ever got that wet from tasting someone. Anthony had it going on.

The head seemed to be my favorite part. Its mushroomed shape fit into my mouth, leaving just enough space for my saliva to slip through. My natural lube made for the perfect job, and Anthony pulsated every time I slid down on it. I took it with my hand and softly shook it. "You like it?"

"Yes."

"Can I ride it?" I asked as I gave him a little hand action.

Anthony, his head still tilted back, didn't answer.

I guess he was enjoying it, so I sped it up a little. "Can I?" I asked again. When he didn't answer that time, I dropped my panties and mounted that big buck. Just as I put the head in, he came.

His moans told me that he hadn't come that good in a long time.

I knew I was working it, but damn! It was over so quick.

"I'm sorry. It's been a long time, and I haven't been with anyone before that was able to bring that out of me so soon after meeting them."

Maybe he was overexcited. Disappointed, I said, "I don't know what to say."

"Do you have a towel or something?" Anthony asked between breaths.

I went into the hall closet and pulled out two hand towels, one for me because he got me a little, and one for him. I tossed it onto his limp penis. After I wiped myself, I put my clothes back on. He hadn't moved yet, so I tapped his foot. "Get cleaned up."

Anthony lifted his head, licked those sexy lips, and thanked me.

I would've loved for him to thank me by getting hard again, but that didn't happen. "You're welcome. I have to go back to DMV and pick up my friend."

Anthony had to go, so I went into the kitchen.

When I came back, he had put himself away and pulled his pants up.

I had planned on spending a few hours with him. I wanted to be fucked but the fact that he came so quickly was a turn-off. I thought about telling him about his self, but he wasn't worth it. The quicker I got him out, the better. "So . . . I'll catch up with you later?"

"All right."

Umph, I don't know. I wasn't used to guys like Anthony. All the men I'd been with had a lot of licks in them and were long-lasting. I could tell that we weren't going to have much in common or be spending that much time together in the near future. What I needed on a consistent basis was to get laid, so I guess I had to stick with Boyfriend and reach out to some of my old flings.

Chapter 7

Lyda

When I picked Boyfriend up at the DMV, he was pissed.

I made it up to him when I took him home and let him tear my ass out the frame.

He ended up spending a few days with me. All we did was fuck, eat, fuck, and eat some more.

"I think I need to go food shopping," I said as I stood in front of the refrigerator.

"Okay, here's some money. I'll chill here, if that's cool." He tossed me a few dollars.

I took his money and left and returned about an hour later. "Baby, come help me with the bags." I walked in the door with a bag in one hand. I saw the stack of mail on the kitchen table and grabbed it as I looked for him in the other room. I walked into our bedroom and caught Boyfriend quickly hanging up the phone. "Who was that?"

"Wrong number. How was your day?" He came over and gave me a kiss.

He smelled good. He always smelled good. He had on his jeans and Timberlands, I loved it when he dressed like that. Boyfriend was thugged out and I loved that, but he was also stupid. Just plain old dumb sometimes. He was also clingy. If he didn't do it to me the way he did, he would've been gone already. I had a few other men that I saw too, but so far Boyfriend was at the top of the "fucking" scale so I had to be nice to him.

When I met him, I was playing the field like crazy. I had boyfriends throughout the entire tri-state area. I would go away for days to spend time with them. My activities had been cut short since I started playing with Boyfriend because he lived the closest and was up my ass ungodly.

I sat on the edge of the bed and took my shoes off. Something told me to look at the caller ID. I saw that Anthony had called. Boyfriend must've answered the phone. I could only imagine what he said. Guess Anthony was pissed and just said wrong number when he heard another man's voice.

I called him back.

"How are you?" he asked.

"Good. What's up?"

"I wanted to know when I could see you again."

"I don't think it's going to work out."

"Why?"

"You know, I just don't and I don't believe in wasting people's time."

"This about me, right?"

I hesitated. "Yes, it is."

"I was a little excited, Lyda."

"I was too, and you were the only one who got yours off."

"I know what you're saying, but damn, give a brother a break."

I thought about it for a minute. "Okay, so when do you want to get together?"

"What are you doing in about an hour?"

"*You* . . . if you're up to the task."

"I'll be there."

"Okay." I hung up the phone and thought for a moment. That meant that I had to get Boyfriend out of there. I went to him. "Baby, listen, I have some things to do, so how about I drop you off and we can hook up tomorrow?"

"I'll go with you."

"No, I'll drop you off."

"Why are you trying to get me out of here so quick?"

"Look, I just want to chill. You know what's up." I'd told him when we met, that we weren't exclusive. *Shit, I got's to get mine.*

"So you need a couple of hours to just do you, huh?" He knew how to talk to me, I liked that shit raw, and he was laying it on me.

"Yeah."

"How many hours before you're gonna want this chocolate dick?"

"Just give me a few; call me later on this evening."

He gave me a kiss on the lips.

On my way back from dropping Boyfriend off, I stopped at the 7-Eleven to get some juice to mix with the vodka that I had at the house. I was in the freezer area and ran into Quincy, an old friend of mine who also broke me off a little something when times were rough.

"Damn, baby, long time no see."

He was sexy as hell. "Right. How you doing?"

"I'm good, baby, you know." He rubbed up against me.

"Oh, okay. So everything's good?"

"Better now. What's good with you?"

"I'm chillin' right now." I started to walk away as I answered him.

"So then what's up? Can we hook up?"

I looked at him. He still looked good. I looked down and noticed that he had a wedding band on. "So when did that happen?" I pointed to his hand.

"Six months ago."

"And you're creeping already?"

"You know how we used to do, Lyda."

"Call me tomorrow, and we'll get together for a drink or something. Right now I have to go." We exchanged numbers and I left.

When I pulled up to the house, Anthony was there, waiting for me. I tried to smile and be optimistic that he'd break me off something good and have some stamina at the same time.

I poured us a drink, and we headed right to the bedroom. Within minutes we were both undressed.

Anthony took me and turned me around. He lifted me up onto the bed and took it from behind. He held my hips tight, and his long strokes were hitting my spot. He was hard as hell. Then he stopped and began licking me from behind. No area from my ass to my pussy went untouched. I didn't know what got into him, but he was working me out.

By the time we finished, I was exhausted. "What has gotten into you?" I asked as I lay on the bed.

"I just wanted you to know what it really is."

"Well, I hope you can keep that going."

He peeked out of the bathroom and shot me a smile with those sexy lips again. *If he keeps this up I could see us sexing each other up on a regular.* But I really wanted to see what Quincy was talking about.

Chapter 8

Valen

"This was a good idea," I said as I ate my fried catfish, yams, and collard greens."

"I can't believe you've never been to Delta's, Valen."

"Jalisa, how can Valen go anywhere when the warden plans her every move?"

"Lyda, he isn't a warden, he's a growth that's killing me inside."

We hadn't been out in a long time. And we were all fed up with the mess that our men were putting us through.

"Roger really feels that he deserves to have me any way he sees. My opinion on our sex life is of no interest to him. He doesn't even kiss me. Hell, he doesn't even look me in the eyes. He looks to the side or closes them all together. No facial expression or anything. Just grunts of satisfaction to him and disgust to me. I feel so humiliated after we have sex. My husband has no desire for me."

Jalisa looked over at me. "That's messed up. Do you think he's cheating on you?" *What? Did she think I was going to keep him doing it to a blow up doll under wraps? Hell no.*

"Roger doesn't cheat. He thinks it's his God-given right to get pleasure any way he wants."

"What does that mean?" Jalisa asked.

"He cheats." Lyda scowled.

"You don't understand, Lyda."

"The hell I don't. I have *men*, not a man, in my life for a reason. They're not interested in making sure we're straight, so I make sure *I'm* straight. Look, he's cheating on you with a life-size Barbie doll. And, girl, he works it, do you hear me? We saw him, didn't we, Jalisa? There, I said it."

"Yes, we did."

I started laughing hysterically.

"What's so funny?" Lyda asked dumbfounded.

"Valen, why are you laughing?"

"I'm laughing because I could only imagine what you guys think you saw. How? When?" I managed to ask between breaths. My eyes were tearing from laughing so hard.

"We went over to your house the other night to see if you wanted to get something to eat. We knocked on the door, and when no one answered we went around back to your bedroom window. And there he was, getting busy with her . . . it . . . whatever."

"Valen, we actually thought it was you. But the thing had long hair, and *hello*, you don't. Super-woman over here," Jalisa pointed at Lyda, "busted the side panel window of the front door and un-locked it so we could get in. Then she pushed me through your bedroom door."

The mood of everyone at the table changed. I wasn't laughing now. "Roger said that he locked himself out of the house. Why didn't you guys tell me this when we were on the phone planning this outing?"

"We thought telling you face-to-face would be better."

I didn't understand that at all. If it were me and I found out something about my girl's man, I think I would tell her right away. That really upset me. "Well, I understand that, but this is serious; I would expect you to tell me right away."

"We did try to call you, Valen," Lyda said.

"You would've preferred a message?"

"No, I wouldn't, but I would at least have ex-pected you to tell me when were on the phone. That's not right."

"We're sorry, Valen," Jalisa said; "we thought we were handling it the right way."

"Sorry, Valen. Ay, girl, I don't think I would be staying around for the reason he will give you when you confront him about it. Lies, they'll be nothing but lies."

"Valen, you don't have to stand for this. You de-serve better; we all do. We need to stop depending on them to make us happy. They don't listen when we talk to them about neglecting us; they think we're nagging. A couple hundred dollars later and they think they've solved the problem. I'm ready to do me. Forget them."

"Pff, that worked for me for a long time with my

ex-men. But now all I want is some slamming sex. I got my own loot. Boyfriend hits me off real good. Anthony, well, I still don't know about him. Our last encounter he held his own. Probably a fluke."

"You guys actually saw Roger having sex with a blow up doll?"

"Girl, he was tearing that booty up," Lyda said.

"Wow! That explains a lot. Why be with me when he could have someone or something that doesn't want or need anything, doesn't talk back or ask questions, doesn't need to be loved, doesn't need to climax, and can be used whenever he wants to use them? I can't believe this."

"Why? Why, Valen, can't you believe that Roger played you out like that? You said it yourself he doesn't talk to you, ask you what you think about anything, or even want you around if you're not waiting on him hand and foot. I mean, we're all guilty of letting them use us, so I agree with Jalisa. We need to take care of ourselves once and for all, no ifs, ands, or buts about it."

"Oh no, I can't cheat on Roger; that's just not something I can do."

"Valen, how long are you going to put up with this?" Jalisa had little sympathy in her voice. "Enough is enough. Why aren't we deserving of being loved? We're in our prime, girl, and I know sometimes I feel like I'm about to explode. It sucks to have a husband who doesn't desire you. Frankly, I'm tired of it. One more chance and that's it. So what's it gonna be, Valen?"

"I can't; I wasn't brought up that way. And don't judge me, Jalisa you're in the same boat."

"Excuse me?"

"You heard me. You complain about the same things I do, and you're still with your man. Have you stepped out on him yet?"

"Damn sure did, and had a ball doing it."

"Oh no, you didn't. And you haven't said anything to us about it? You are so wrong, and you do have a lot of nerve."

"It just happened; it wasn't a big deal."

"Okay. Well, we'll get to that in a minute. Valen, were you brought up to be used? Were you brought up to be disrespected and ignored by the man who you said 'I do' to? Are you the only one who has to "do"? Bump that! You better snap out of it; Roger is not going to change."

"You know, Lyda, you're right. I know he isn't going to change, I just have a hard time accepting it."

"Well, you can get used to the idea better if you were fucking someone else while you pondered if you wanted to stay with his sorry ass. It would definitely help you decide . . . especially if the dick is good."

I looked at Lyda. I had to admit that although she got what she needed from several different men, she did seem the happiest out of the three of us. Lyda could be blunt, but I admired her honesty and aggressiveness when it came to getting what she wanted.

Then Jalisa looked at me. "Let me ask you a question, Valen where were you the night we came over to your house?"

"On the way to pick up some golf clubs Roger ordered. I got a flat on 18."

"How long have you been complaining to him to replace your balding tires?"

"I guess for as long as I've been complaining to you guys that he hasn't replaced them yet."

"Exactly."

"Are they replaced yet?" Lyda asked.

"No. The AAA guy replaced just the one tire that got a flat."

"Don't you get it? He knew it was a matter of time until one of them blew. He took his chances and sent you on a ride so that he could play with plastic chick. He's dissing you left and right *and* you still have three bald, ready-to-blow tires. Bet you he's home doing it to her, or it, right now."

Jalisa shook her head at Lyda.

"She's right, Jalisa. I've had it."

"Okay. So then what are we going to do? Personally, I'm done complaining," Jalisa said.

"Get the dick!" Lyda blurted.

"Get the dick!" I repeated. "Get the dick, get the dick, get the dick!"

Chapter 9

Lyda

On my way home, I thought about our conversation at dinner. I was so glad that I wasn't married. Valen and Jalisa were bound by law to their men. I almost wanted to give them my book of phone numbers and let them run wild with it, but neither of them would've ever done that. Besides, they wouldn't have wanted any man I'd been with, especially since there was a possibility that I'd hook up with one of them again.

I took a shower, dried off, and put on a pair of sweats and a T-shirt. I went and grabbed the bills and sat on the couch to go through them when the phone rang. "What's up, Quincy? I didn't expect your call this soon."

"I know, but I'm really anxious to catch up on old times."

"Really? And how are you going to get out, with

your wife, who I'm sure wants to know your every move?"

"Let *me* worry about that. Can I come through now?"

"Sure. Do you remember where I live?

"Yes."

"I'll be here."

J'adore was my perfume of choice at the time, so I sprayed a squirt or two, fluffed my hair, changed into something more appropriate, and was ready.

Within a half an hour Quincy was there.

"That was quick. Where were you calling from?"

"Around the corner." He tossed his keys on the table, walked up to me, and gave me a kiss.

I took his tongue and sucked it.

"Damn, girl! Still got that sucking thing down, huh?"

"Mmm hmm."

Quincy guided his hand down to my pussy. He fingered me then brought his finger up to his mouth and sucked my wetness off. "You're bitter."

"You like it though." I pulled back. "Meet me in the bedroom." I went into the bathroom and closed the door. I touched myself and smelled my finger. I had a faint odor. It didn't smell bad, but it wasn't my usual smell either. I wet a washcloth with warm water, washed my pussy again, then returned to Quincy. When I got into the bedroom, he was standing butt naked at the end of the bed masturbating. "Wow, Quincy!" I'd never seen him do that. "I like. I like."

"Aw, that's sweet. No interruptions. That's what I'm talking about."

I floated up against him. "I want you so much," I whispered in his ear as I peeked at the clock.

"I want you too."

I pushed him onto the bed, knelt in front of him, and took him in my mouth. He was hard as a rock. His mushroom-shaped head was tight as I put my lips around it. I loved to taste him, and the fact that he was so excited got me even more excited. I climbed on top of him and slowly guided him into me. "Baby, what's gotten you so hard?"

"Thinking about your last lick."

I slowly moved my hips in a winding motion so that I could make sure I got all of him. I closed my eyes and imagined us together in the woods on a rainy night.

Quincy took my nipple in his mouth and slowly flicked it with his tongue.

I was loving him at that moment. I picked up the pace of my lovemaking and then squatted over him. I held onto his shoulders and bucked him so hard, my thighs began to burn.

Quincy's intense facial expression told me that he thoroughly enjoyed what I was doing to him. He held me so tight; then all of a sudden he came to a halt. "Get up for a minute, baby." He reached over to his pants and pulled out a condom.

I appreciated him doing that; after all, he did have a wife. As I stood there waiting for him to put it on, I began to smell that faint odor again. He must not have smelled it, so I didn't say anything. I just mounted him again and finished what we had started.

Quincy left about an hour or so later. I expected

him to be more aggressive but was satisfied. I finished going through my bills then fell asleep on the couch.

The following morning, I was still on the couch. I looked up at the clock and it was 8:30. I got up, put some coffee on, and got in the shower. While I was in the shower, I douched. I didn't smell the odor, but I just wanted to clean it out, "pussy issues" was the last thing I needed or wanted. I grabbed my robe, made a cup of coffee, and plopped right back on the couch. I fell back asleep and was awakened by the doorbell.

"Who is it?" I tightened the belt to my robe and peeked through the peephole.

"It's Anthony."

I didn't recall telling him that he could stop by without calling. I opened the door. "Did you call?" I asked. "Because if you did, I didn't hear the phone ring." I let him in.

"No. Actually, I was just in the neighborhood and thought I'd stop by and see what you were up to."

"I was laying down. I fell asleep watching television."

"Well, maybe I'll come back another time."

I turned and looked at him. I wanted him to stay and possibly give me some of that good dick he gave me before. "Nah, you can stay awhile. I'll make some breakfast."

After I cooked and cleaned up the mess, Anthony and I were in the bedroom getting it in. He was laying on the bed while I sucked his dick. I thought about Quincy and our sex from the night before, and that made be suck Anthony with more intensity.

"Damn, girl suck this dick." He held my head in place as I glided up and down.

Anthony guided me on how fast or slow he wanted.

I loved what he was doing. It got me wet as hell. I sucked as he grabbed my hair.

He held on tighter, and I sucked harder.

"You like it?" I asked.

"Hell yeah! Ride it."

I got up and turned away from Anthony. I straddled him and sat on his dick. I went to work and immediately smelled that odor again. As I was riding him, I turned to see if Anthony smelled it too. He didn't seem to, so I just kept riding.

No sooner did I turn back around than Anthony stopped.

I got up and looked at him. He lay there with the weirdest look on his face. I paced the floor. *This was the second time he did this.* Giving Anthony the benefit of the doubt wasn't working; I just couldn't do it any more. "Anthony."

He lifted his head up slightly and peeped through one eye.

I stood there with my hands on my hips. Once again, Anthony platinum-plated the term "minute man." Disgust draped my face. I couldn't hide it any longer. I let his ass have it. "Sit up, please."

"Why? What's wrong?" He shifted himself to scratch.

"I can't take the little action that you're trying to give. This few minutes of having sex isn't working for us. The last time we were together you were on point; now it's like the first time we were together, you gotta go."

"What? Just a minute ago you were riding me like crazy."

"Yes, I was because I thought that you were going to be in it to win it, but I guess I was wrong."

"I don't know what to say. Part of me is pissed and feel like you have some nerve, but then the other part of me feels like you should thank me for getting it on with you."

"Thank you? What the hell is that supposed to mean?"

He got up and went over to the side of the bed. He bent down and picked up his pants.

As he put them on, I drilled him even further. "Anthony, what the fuck you talking about?"

"Lyda, you're a pretty girl I'll give you that but not many dudes would put up with that."

"You're making me laugh. What exactly do you put up with?" I shifted from one foot to the other.

"Can you hand me my shirt?" he said with a cocky attitude.

I was getting real pissed. I reached over to the chair that sat in the corner right behind me, grabbed his shirt, and tossed over to him. "Well, spit it out already."

"Are you sure you want to have this conversation? I mean no one is perfect, and I'm willing to accept you with your faults. Can you accept me with mine or what you consider to be my faults?"

"You know what, Anthony if you were a real man, it wouldn't take you this long to say what you have to say. Obviously you don't believe what you think to be my fault; otherwise you wouldn't hesitate to bring it to my attention. What about me could have you so rattled that you can't control yourself from coming like you're twelve years old?"

"Lyda, you stink!"

"Excuse me?" I know this limp dick, shriveled-up-nuts bastard didn't just tell me that I smelled.

"You heard me. Your personal hygiene has a lot to be desired. And before you go complaining about my dick getting soft before you get yours off, try douching every now and then."

"Oh no, you didn't. You weren't saying that when I let you play in it the other day. And if it's that bad, why you keep coming back for more? Huh? You're just mad because I told you your dick done did you dirty and is deemed defective."

"Yeah, okay. When the smell comes looming out, it's not good any more. It almost smells like a wet rag that's been sitting on the corner of the bathtub so long that it dried out and has little fuzzy things on it. *Ewwww!*" He shook in disgust.

Now it was my turn to not know what to say. Anthony just coldblasted me by telling me my coochie stunk. He must've smelled it before and just didn't say anything. Boyfriend never mentioned anything. Quincy said I was bitter but not that I smelled. Even though I knew Anthony was right, he wasn't going to get that off in my house. "Your stroke is for shit. In fact, you don't even have a stroke, you have a strike—out, that is. That's right, you can't fuck. Why is that, Anthony? Am I too much woman for you? Too wild, perhaps, and more comfortable with my body and sexuality than you will ever be? Tell me, did daddy tell you that you were a bad boy all the time?" I put on my best antagonistic impression of a whiny baby.

"Lyda, I'm serious. You stink. I thought that maybe you had a few bad days or you were just coming off of your menstrual, but for real, you need to get that checked out."

"The only thing that needs to get checked out is you. I'm getting ready to take a shower. By the time I get out, I want your punk ass out of here." I turned around, went into the bathroom, and slammed the door behind me.

As I washed up, I realized how embarrassed I was. He wasn't lying. I smelled it myself. Whatever was wrong, I needed to get to my doctors *pronto* to get it right. Anthony had some damn nerve, telling me that I was ripe. But that was okay.

I called my gynecologist the minute he left so I could check things out and make sure he wasn't just mad because of what I said about his dick.

Chapter 10

Jalisa

I stood over the bed and looked at the outfit that I'd planned on wearing for Quinton, a white lace-lined Italian silk sequined halter dress with pink and silver shimmers intertwined throughout. I'd saved it for a special occasion, and it was time to put it to good use. Three buttons were delicately placed at the center, right below the breasts, for quick and easy access. The matching shoes were clear with a sequined four-inch heel. The entire outfit was sharp.

After my conversation with Valen and Lyda, I wasn't wearing anything for his butt. *He can forget about me trying to make it right between us, I'm done.* Then the phone call came. Quinton called to tell me that he was working a double.

Ordinarily, I would've been pissed, but that day, I could care less. I still had to talk mess anyway, just so he knew where I was with the entire situation.

"Well, what's new, Quinton? You've worked a double two to three times a week for the last month."

"Jalisa, what do you want me to do? I had to hire new people, and who else would train them? I wanted them trained a certain way. My restaurant has a reputation to protect, and the only way I can be sure things are going smoothly is if I'm here looking over everyone."

"Well, how long is this going to go on? I mean it seems like ever since we spoke you've been avoiding me. Is that the case?" I had to whine a little.

"No. I just have to work."

"Okay."

I decided to go down to the restaurant and have dinner. Wear my little sexy dress and let everybody see what I was working with. I was horny as hell and in need of some serious "boning."

"Rub all of this with this soap. Put a little squirt of something and go and get me a man." I washed up thoroughly because, if I had it my way, Quinton would smell me once and want me on the spot. But hell if he thought he was going to get any.

The restaurant was packed. I must admit, it was elegantly decorated. The staff was dressed in all black uniforms that kind of looked like they were tailor-made. I walked up to the reservation booth, where a fine, young brother stood, marking off what I assumed were already occupied tables. He was looking down. His hairline was neat, and his goatee was perfectly aligned.

I lightly tapped on the podium.

He promptly lifted his head up.

Oh my, call the wam-bu-lance. I'm about to have a

heart attack. He could be no more than twenty years old and was fine as hell. "May I have a table for one please?" I asked him.

"Yes, ma'am." He grabbed a menu and instructed me to follow him.

He led me to a table that was secluded by a Chinese room divider. Its transparent panels made it very intimate. In the middle of the table there was a lavender candle surrounded with white rose petals at the base. Pewter napkin holders studded with cherubs playing violins held the linen napkins in place. He turned to face me. "Will this do?" He gently smiled.

"Yes. What is your name?" I couldn't help asking; I felt an attraction to him the minute I laid eyes on him.

"Darrell, ma'am." An innocent look draped his mocha-complexioned face. Long eyelashes complemented his hazel eyes. He had a slim build, and from his broad shoulders hung muscular arms. His waist should've been in the Guinness Book of World Records, it was so small was tight. His butt looked firm as if he was maybe a football player or worked out on a daily basis. Either way, baby boy had it going on.

Darrell was a cutie. If I had to guess, he stood about six feet, give or take an inch. His hair was thick with curly locks and faded right above the ears, which gave the appearance of a short Afro. I was really feeling his shy demeanor and his taut physique. Now, I'd never robbed the cradle, but there was always a first time for everything.

Darrell pulled out the chair, and I sat down, never taking my eyes off him.

"And what wine will you be having? I will be sure to have it brought to you right away."

"Why? Why can't you serve it to me?" I asked, almost offended.

"Because . . . I'm really a server; I'm covering for another hostess who called out from work this evening. So I'm not serving tonight."

"I see." I flirtatiously twisted my hair. I wasn't mad. *I could do a bus boy.* "Tell you what, I'll go to the bar and order my drink myself. I can bring it back to my table; I don't have a problem with that. And, Darrell, thank you." I puckered my lips, lowered my gaze onto his body, and sashayed over to the lounge area.

I was a bit overdressed, but that was okay. I was on a mission to break this curse that had plagued Quinton and me with stale sex and slighted kinship. Tonight was going to reveal what we were made of. I'd never done anything like this before and was at my wit's end; my spontaneity ended when Quinton stopped showing me affection.

"May I have a Cosmopolitan, please?"

"Sure. With Hangar Orange or Absolut Raspberry?"

"Surprise me," I purred to the bartender. It was open season on everybody, but baby Darrell really caught my attention.

The drink was strong and had me feeling tingly. I got a buzz before I finished half the damn thing. The thought of Quinton seeing me dressed like this made me want to roar like a lioness. It was turning me on. And Darrell added to the aura of lustfulness that had so graciously placed itself upon me. *With any luck, I'll be getting my Darrell on!*

I ordered the almond-crusted salmon with pota-
toes and sautéed spinach and was very impressed.
From the looks of the restaurant, his service staff,
and the food, maybe he needed to be here for
everything to flow as nicely as it did. Maybe I
should've stepped into his world and spend more
time with him at the restaurant, helping out wher-
ever I could.

To be perfectly honest, since he opened it up
about six months ago, I really hadn't been there to
help him and didn't really show any interest in it.
And besides the fact that I was busy with my own
business, he never really invited me there, come to
think of it. That probably bothered him and he
just didn't say anything.

The waiter brought me a tray of desserts to se-
lect from. I politely declined to sample the peach
amaretto cheesecake, triple chocolate-layered
cake with white chocolate rinds, or the flan. "I really
wish I could, but I have to watch my figure. But you
know what, can you bring me another Cosmopolitan?"

"Of course." He turned away and left.

I felt invigorated. My impetuous decision to show
up here gave me the feeling of living on the edge,
something I never did. Everything in my life was on
a schedule and systematically planned to a *T*.

When Quinton opened the restaurant, our time
together was cut in half. I too had just started my
tailoring business. While Quinton studied for his
managerial course, it was easy for me to cut right
there on the living room floor while he read his
books. Those nights were great. When we tired, he
of studying and I of sewing, we would make some

tea and cuddle up on the couch for a break. We wouldn't talk; we would just feel each other's vibe and know we were in love. It was understood that we had each other's backs and that it was us until the end.

Lately however, I was feeling empty. Late nights at the office brought me home tired, and his doubles at the restaurant brought him home even later. Even if I tried to stay up and wait for him, almost always, I'd be asleep by the time he came through the door.

"Here you go, ma'am."

"Thank you. Is Quinton here?" And the last time we spoke, he couldn't leave the restaurant, yet I hadn't seen him all night.

"Quinton has left the restaurant. He left word with the front desk that he had an errand to run."

I guess the look on my face told him that I wasn't happy with the news that he'd just given me.

"Would you like to leave a message for him?" he asked apprehensively.

"No, thank you. I'm Jalisa, Quinton's wife."

"How nice!" He turned his head and flipped his eyes to the sky.

"Well, all right then," I sighed to myself. *Where could Quinton have gone? He told me he had to be here to keep things under control. What could be more important than the restaurant? Maybe he ran out of something and needed to get some more.* I finished my drink and waited for him to return.

An hour passed and still no Quinton. My patience had run out; I was ready to go home. I got up and left the restaurant. As soon as I got in the car, I called Quinton on his cell phone. "Quinton, where are you?"

"I'm at the restaurant."

"No, you're not. I was just there. The waiter said that you left and would be right back. Why are you lying?"

"Who was the waiter?"

"I didn't get his name. He was rude, though, once I told him who I was. Answer my question, Quinton. Why are you lying?"

"I'm not lying Jalisa and that would be Wesley; he doesn't mean any harm to any of the customers."

"First of all, I'm not just a customer, I'm your wife. And when I told him that, he should've acted more appropriately. Secondly, I could give a damn about Wesley. He said you left and you said you didn't, why would he lie?"

"Jalisa, what is the big deal? That's Wesley's personality. Why are you calling me with this?"

"I was calling you to see where you were. I thought I would come have dinner and that you'd join me for a few minutes."

"You know I can't do that; I have a restaurant to run."

"You are so lame. You and your excuses are getting on my last nerve. It never fails that you have an excuse, any excuse, as to why you can't spend any time with me."

"I trained the night manager all week. She picked up on everything nicely, so tonight won't be a late night. I should be home around one o'clock. Damn, Jalisa!"

"'One o'clock'? Don't bother, Quinton. You know what . . . you're going to mess around and somebody will be all up in this booty." I hung up the phone. Quinton was forever acting like I was so dramatic. He got on my nerves with that.

Quinton never debated whether or not he left the restaurant. In fact, he switched the conversation to Wesley and my overreacting. Wesley may have been lying, but why? Obviously he didn't know me from the next chick that came there dressed in a hot nightgown looking for their husband. Something didn't seem right about that.

I was beginning to give myself a headache, thinking about Quinton and his nonsense. It was 12:45 and he would be home shortly. Those Cosmopolitans had me ripe and ready for some type of action. When I got home, I brushed my teeth, removed the little makeup I had applied, turned on the radio, and got in the bed. I fluffed both of our pillows and gently fell back, still wearing my sexy outfit.

As I lay there, I remembered the day that I met Quinton. The ice-cream store was our first encounter. Come to think of it, I hadn't had a sundae like that since. I jumped out of bed. I had a brain-child. "I'm going to make me a sundae." I went to the kitchen and looked for whatever I could throw together to make a sundae. We always had fruit in the house, so that wasn't a problem. I went to the refrigerator and looked for whipped cream. Then I reached into the freezer and grabbed the ice-cream. I searched for the largest platter I had and went to work.

Once I was finished, I stared at it. There was

something missing. "A cherry!" I went back to the refrigerator. No cherries. So I went to the cabinets. Nothing there either. I needed something to put on top. Then I remembered that Lyda and Jalisa had given me a tube of edible cinnamon body gel. I ran upstairs and grabbed it from the box it had come in. On my way back downstairs, I squeezed a small amount of it on the tip of my finger. "Eh, it will do." I put a dot the size of a nickel on top of the whipped cream and swirled it to a point. "Perfect!" I grabbed a spoon.

As I carried my creation upstairs to my bedroom, I thought of how back in the day this would've meant so much. I did Lyda's little pump dance to the nightstand on my side of the bed and set the platter down. I scooped up a strawberry, dipped it in the whipped cream, and slowly chewed it. "Yes, this is what I'm talking about." I hopped back in the bed and positioned myself so I could just reach and scoop and eat.

The softness of the sheets was a turn-on. I unbuttoned my dress and pulled out my breasts so that they sat like two ready-to-be-picked mangos. My nipples were hard. I gently grabbed one as I parted my legs and touched my passion fruit. Slowly, I made tiny circles on my clit. I had thoughts of Quinton licking my wetness. He held on tight to my thighs to ensure that he got as deep as he could, which would surely make me climax. His face was covered with my juices. I looked down and thought, *Yes, Quinton, please keep loving me.* Minutes of him devouring my love would take me a step closer to losing my mind. I took my legs and pulled them up by my ankles, giving Quinton the queue that it was time. Time for him to enter my hot, raging inferno. But he wasn't finished tasting my delight.

Words of seduction rolled off his tongue between the lashings of my clit. *Damn, you looked so sexy in that dress tonight. I'd never seen such a beautiful and desirable woman like you before. You wanted me, didn't you? I could tell when you looked me in my eyes.*

Yes, I did. I want you now.

I felt him stop. I looked down, and there he was. His face was soaked with my honeydew, and his eyes were mysterious. We both looked at each other as if we had done something wrong. However, nothing was against either his will or mine; it was what we both wanted.

"Darrell," I moaned. My movements were tight and had purpose. I wanted to cum. I needed a release, and Darrell was my mental seducer. Images of us making love in different places in the restaurant danced in my head. First, it was on the piano that sat beside the bar. Then it was in the bathroom stall. And lastly, on Quinton's desk, which had papers stacked neatly on it. Darrell was hitting it so hard, Quinton's papers were all over the damn place.

As I wound my hips, I felt the intensity of my pent-up frustration, and before I knew it, I squirted. "Oh my God." My body jerked like I was possessed, and I made sounds that I never knew I could make. I hugged myself as the feeling went from my head to my toes, making me jerk in satisfaction. My thighs and the sheets were soaked with my warm juices. I touched myself as I came down from my climax.

Moments later, I fell into a serene and euphoric

state of sleep. Even when Quinton and I had good sex, I never came the way I just did—ever. And to think it was made even more intense when my thoughts switched from Quinton to Darrell.

Chapter 11

Valen

I felt like a damn fool when Lyda and Jalisa told me that they'd busted Roger having sex with a blow up doll. I was humiliated beyond belief. And they were right, Roger didn't care anything about my well-being. I should've known when I told him I wanted to have children and he rejected the idea out of hand.

"Children aren't in my plans. I have a lot on my plate right now between drafting and dealing with everyday issues and you."

"And *me*? What do you mean by that?"

"You require a lot of attention. You say you want children. You'll have to share me with them."

"What would I be sharing? It's not like you show me any affection. I can do without our calculated sex. Maybe a child would be good for us, you know . . . add to our lives."

"Valen, my life is fine. And what do you have to

be angry about? I provide you with everything you need. You don't have to pay one bill in this house, and on top of that, I give you an allowance of three hundred a week to do with as you please. Is that not enough? Do you need more?"

I was convinced that Roger wasn't capable of giving me anything more. He was okay with providing me with a house, which to me wasn't home. These four walls were filled with nothing but emptiness. Because he gave me money, he thought he could withhold any emotional commitment and that I didn't need it. A purse or a new wardrobe should suffice.

I was to blame in part. I allowed him to dictate my every move, from quitting my job as a bank manager to canceling my gym membership because *he* thought the money he gave me could be better spent.

"I don't see a difference in you. Why do you put so much time into the gym when you don't get any results?"

Now, he further demeaned me and chose a plastic doll over me. Why didn't he just divorce me? If he was so much out of love with me, why not let me go? Surely I could handle a one-time crisis better than the daily torture of feeling unworthy. I knew that I was worthy of being loved.

But Roger was perfectly happy with the wall that he built between us. I didn't have the energy to fight with him or even fight with myself and ask how something like this could've happened.

I went into the garage, hoping that he had enough sense to at least keep "resuscitator Annie" out of the house, to lessen the chances of my finding it while I was cleaning or something. I ripped through the cabinets of army clothing and garage sale items and found nothing. I went outside and into the shed where he kept all of his personal items and again found nothing.

"When does he have the time to clean this place? It's immaculate." There wasn't a dust bunny in sight. I spent another few minutes looking through his things but came up with absolutely nothing. I made sure I left everything the way I found it so that he wouldn't know I went through his things; I wanted to be a little more careful than he was. I trucked myself back into the house.

Roger also felt it necessary not to tell me where he went and what time he planned on coming back, so I had to move quickly and find this "plastic chick," which seemed to have it going on more than I did.

I searched the house from the kitchen pantry to the spare bedroom's walk-in closet. There wasn't a hanger that I didn't inspect, looking for his deflated friend. When I found nothing there, I went in the bathroom and pulled everything from under the sink. No plastic chick.

I went into the master bedroom. "Humph, now that I know there's been some funky mess going on in here, I can feel the foulness," I said to myself as I began in Roger's closet. His closet was the size of a small bedroom and had racks professionally installed for his clothes when we bought the house.

I very carefully went through each of his suits. *It would be easy for him to deflate her and hang her under a pair of slacks.* I was getting grossed out by the thought of him having sex with a piece of plastic.

When I found nothing, I stood in the middle of his closet. I began to feel a lump form in my throat, and my eyes began to water. I hadn't cried in a long time. My emotions had been in hiatus for months now.

I covered my face with my hands. I didn't want to cry, even though I was home alone. I thought the walls would somehow tell Roger that he had me at my lowest with his last stunt. Feeling defeated, I sat on the bed, fell back, and closed my eyes. Nothing appeared. I was literally living in a state of darkness. Then it hit me. I sprung up and lifted up the bed skirt. There was the bitch that got to have sex with my husband, in the plastic flesh. She was folded up haphazardly in a box marked "applications." "Seems he had just about as much respect for her as he did me." I pulled her out. I unfolded her and lay her on the bed. On her clothing, you could see cum spots all over her where Roger had released himself. "Nasty bastard!"

I went back under the bed to see what else I could find. There was a dark, long-haired wig the same length and color as Jalisa's hair. I got upset again as I flung the wig onto the bed. I also found a pair of army boots, a camouflage outfit, and a tube of KY Warming Gel, strawberry flavor. "He has got to be kidding me."

I pulled her out to the garage. I turned on his air pump and inflated her. Then I took her back into the house and sat her at the kitchen table. She was falling out of the chair, so I got some twine and tied her to it. I put her wig on, took off the clothes that he had her dressed in, and dressed her in one of my favorite outfits. I did her makeup.

I even put my new Coach pumps on her and let her sport the matching conductor hat. "There."

It was 5:30, and Roger would be coming home soon. Me and plastic chick were waiting for his simple ass.

I remember when I used to wait for him to come home. When I worked, I would get home about an hour before him and would have a hot meal waiting every night. Eventually, he began coming home with fast food and stopped eating what I cooked. When I stopped cooking, it didn't seem to bother him at all, it just gave him another reason to eat somewhere else.

Chapter 12

Valen

Two hours later, Roger pulled up. I was reading the newspaper and tapping on the table with a pen. My nerves were going crazy. I had anxiety up the wazoo, and that diarrhea feeling was coming on. I was reading the "personals" section because I figured, since I'd be single soon, I needed to know who was looking for what out there. "Hum, what's this?" I came across an ad—*DATES NEEDED FOR COMPANIONSHIP AND FUN. NO STRINGS ATTACHED.*

I circled the ad and folded the paper in half as Roger came through the door. Plastic chick and I were waiting at the dining room table. I heard him toss his keys in the plate by the front door. I made sure his lover was straight then took my seat.

The look on Roger's face was classic.

"Say hi to my friend." I folded my hands under my chin.

"Valen—"

"Don't start with your lies, Roger."

"It's not what you think." He pulled the chair and sat at the table.

"Roger, I don't think anything but that you're a retarded imbecile. You send me out to the boondocks to get you some stupid golf clubs and my girlfriends bust you doing it in the butt to *her*." I pointed to plastic chick. "Was it good, Roger? Tell me, did she stay wet? Do you enjoy the fact that she doesn't require anything from you and your sorry dick? Oh, but wait, she and I talked, and we did agree on one thing, it ain't good, Roger. This is it."

I got up and went into the bedroom and came back with my .45 and popped plastic chick right between the eyes. One of the three bullets I pulled off landed in my cherry oak armoire; the second one hit one of Roger's awards that hung on the wall; and the third was embedded in the door.

"Have you lost your gotdam mind, Valen?" Roger spoke through clenched teeth. "You better come back to reality real quick."

"Roger, the reality is that you don't scare me with your tight jaws. You need to know that the chances of you ever getting to the middle of this 'tootsie' again are slim to none, just like your dick."

"You have been hanging around with Jalisa and Lyda too much. They got you thinking you're all miss high and mighty. Tell me . . . you haven't worked in how long? The only source of income you have is what I give you. What's a girl to do, should I decide to cut that in half or, better yet, off completely?"

"Well, I guess I'd have to get a job, Roger."

"Then I suggest you get to looking."

Chapter 13

Lyda

I was so glad when the doctor's office called me back first thing the next morning and was able to squeeze me in at nine o'clock. I guess they'd heard the urgency in my voice.

Dr. Soreno was fine. You know how most men gynecologists were your "average Joes"? Not mine. His salt and pepper hair gave him a distinguished look. And not only could he dress his ass off, he could give you a look that would make you want to drop your uterus right on his lap to do with it as he pleased, stuff it with his seeds so you could bear his children, whatever he wanted.

"Dr. Soreno will see you now." The nurse opened the door and held it for me to go in. "You'll be in room three. He'll be right in, but first I want to ask you a few questions. What brings you here today?"

"Well, I just want to be sure about my 'area.'"

"Okay. Is there something going on that makes

you think there is something wrong with your area?"

"My boyfriend told me that I had kind of a smell going on. Now, I do use the scented monthly products, but that's it. I don't just insert too many things, you know."

"Of course. Have you noticed the smell? Have you been experiencing any discharge, or does it hurt when you have sex?"

"I did notice the smell a little, but no, no discharge. We had an argument, and he threw that in my face as a reason why he gets soft so quickly."

"Oh my. Well, take this gown and put it on. Doctor will be with you shortly."

I went into the little room and pulled the curtain. I got undressed, put the robe on, and hopped on top of the table. There was a magazine laying on the counter, so I picked it up and began to read as I waited for Dr. Soreno.

A few moments later he came strolling in. "Hello, Lyda."

Damn it! Why couldn't he be my man? "Hi, Dr. Soreno. How've you been?"

"Fine, thank you. And you?"

"Good. No complaints." I really wanted to tell him that my ex-boyfriend had a dick that couldn't perform, and could he hook a sistah up?

"Very well. What brings you here today?"

"Please don't make me say it again. Could you please read the nurse's notes."

He took a moment to review the notes in my file. Although Dr. Soreno had been my doctor for many years now, I still felt uncomfortable having to come and see him about this.

"I know that I'm good, Dr. Soreno, but I just want you to make sure that everything is, you know." I gave him two thumbs-up.

"Of course. Lay back and put your feet into the stirrups." He snapped on a pair of rubber gloves, squeezed a dollop of ointment on his fingers, and inserted them into my vagina. He pressed on my abdomen, searching for any abnormalities, and felt my tubes. "Everything feels okay, but I do smell the odor. I'd like to get a pap smear."

"Okay."

Dr. Soreno buzzed for the nurse, and she came in and watched as he performed the pap. That big silver thing that he inserted would've been better received if it needed double D batteries and he was the one buzzing with me.

I probably shouldn't have been thinking about him like that at the time. I let out a sigh of relief when it was out.

"All done. Get dressed, and I'll see you in my office."

"Okay, Dr. Soreno."

He and the nurse left me to get dressed. When I was done, I went to his office.

"It's going to take a few days to get the test results back, but here is a prescription for penicillin, take it for the next five days, and be sure to finish it all. And no scented anything up there . . . understand?"

"Yes, I understand. What do you think it is?" *Witcho' fine ass.*

"A yeast infection, I saw a little discharge; the test will tell all."

"Thanks, Dr. Soreno." I turned and walked out of the office.

When I got home there were two messages on my phone. I walked over to the answering machine and pressed play.

You have two new messages. First new message: Beep. Lyda, it's Anthony. I want to talk. Call me when you get this message. Message deleted.

Next new message: Beep. Lyda, ay, it's your boo. Let me dip this chocolate stick. Holla at yo' boy.

"Jackass number two. Boy, I sure can pick 'em."

Chapter 14

Jalisa

It was around four in the morning when I woke up and noticed that Quinton wasn't in bed. I felt like I slept an entire eight hours. I got up and changed the sheets. I still couldn't believe what I'd experienced a few hours ago. It was amazing to me what you can do if your mind was in the right place.

I dragged the sheets down to the laundry, which was located beside the kitchen. The lights were on in the den, and I could hear music playing. I stuck my head in and there was Quinton. "Golf? Since when have you been playing golf?"

"I took it up a few weeks ago. I saw Roger out one day, and he invited me to join him and his buddies for a game," he said in a cold voice.

Quinton and Roger were on a hi-and-bye basis. Their interaction was news to me and would be to

Valen too, I was sure. "Roger? Okay, since when have you and Roger been so close, or close enough for him to ask you to play golf?"

"Well, with all the hours I put in at work, I could use a 'vice' to relax, get my mind off of things." He gently swung the golf club.

I was fuming. "Wow! You can put time into learning a new vice and completely ignore the fact that we need more time together?"

"Jalisa, do you ever let up? All you do is nag. It always has to be about you. Maybe if you would shut your trap for a minute, we could move past this slump we're in. I get tired of you always complaining about what you don't have. I provide you with everything you need, you have your own money that I don't ask a penny of. Your business is good, isn't it? So what the hell is the problem? Get off a brother's back!"

Well, you know fire was coming out of my ass right then. "Okay, Quinton," was all I said as I continued on my way to the laundry room. That was it for me. Quinton didn't have to worry about me nagging him about anything else any more.

On my way back to bed, I said, "Quinton, I think your restaurant business is doing great, and the food was delicious. I think I'll frequent it more often. Good night or morning."

Quinton had crawled into bed shortly after I did. He made sure not to touch me, which was fine by me.

I lay there thinking about Darrell and his cute self. I wondered how old he was and thought, *I'll find out soon enough.* I lay down for an hour or two more.

When eight o'clock rolled around, I hopped out of bed. Steven was due in to pick up his shirts at ten that morning. I had them sent out to my girl in California this time because I was trying to open up some time for Quinton, and since Steven was a regular, all I had to do was send her his updated measurements. And if they needed any alterations, I'd do them on the spot in my office.

I went into the bathroom and closed the door behind me. I ran a hot, steamy shower and got in. Darrell popped into my mind. The water trickled off my erect nipples, which he sucked dry. I fell back against the cold tile and began to play with my clit and moaned in sheer arousal as fire brewed from my desire to be fucked by him. Then he took me into his mouth as I spread my legs, my shaven lips calling for him to enter me. "Mmmm," I softly whispered. Within minutes, I came. I didn't know if I was still hot from the previous night's climax or what, but I was good with it.

I washed up, washed my hair, and got out. I wrapped a towel around me and wiped the steam off of the mirror. When my eyes met their reflection, I gave myself two thumbs-up.

Steven was on time. He waited outside the door that led to my office, two cups of coffee in his hands. "Well, good morning. Don't we look absolutely fabulous today."

"Thank you, Steven. And you look great as usual too. Come on up."

When we got up to my office, I opened the

blinds and turned on the radio. *A little soft jazz to suit the mood.* "Have a seat, Steven."

He handed me the coffee.

"Thank you. That was so thoughtful. I didn't even have time to make a cup; it's just what I need. I have your shirts. Would you like to try them on? I can do any alterations right now."

"Yes, I'll try them on in a few. Let's catch up. How are things with you and your husband?"

"To tell you the truth, Steven, they haven't gotten any better. I tried to talk with Quinton again and got nowhere. In fact, he's taken up a new pastime, a 'vice,' as he so puts it."

"Really? And what is that?"

"Golf."

"Golf?"

"Mmm hmm, golf. He said that he's going with my girlfriend's husband. Valen's husband and Quinton were never close like that. Guess things change, huh? Yeah, right."

"So even after you spoke to him about your concerns, he still didn't address them?"

"Oh yeah, he addressed them." I sat my coffee on the table and went to get Steven's shirts. "He told me that I'm a nag and everything ain't about me and that if I would shut my mouth long enough, maybe things would change."

"I can't believe that. That's amazing to me. I mean, if my wife were to come to me with that, I would at least try and give her a little of what she wanted. That's where a lot of men go wrong. They don't realize that they don't have to go overboard. Normally when a woman says that she feels neglected, all she's looking for is attention. Am I right?"

"Yes, you are so right. I don't want him to lose himself in me, but damn! We are married. Can I get a little something, some of the time?"

Steven looked at me. I was sure he remembered the conversation we had when he'd made it perfectly clear that, if I needed anything, he would be there for me.

"Well, let's get you fitted. Take off your shirt."

Steven obliged. His arms were so muscular. His "wife-beater" t-shirt fit him perfectly, showing his firm chest and abs. It was neatly tucked into his khaki pants and finished off with a gator belt.

"Put this one on."

He turned, and I lifted the shirt up as he slid his arms into it. I watched as he buttoned it up. I was getting aroused by his smooth movements. He tucked the shirt into his pants then moved a little to find his comfort level. "I think it's a little big in this area." He pointed to his torso. "The shirt hangs over the belt too much. It's too baggy. Maybe you can take it in so that it's more fitted against my waist."

"Okay." I reached for my pinball. "You'll need to take your pants down so that I could see how tight you want it."

"I like it tight," he said, flirting. Steven pulled down his pants.

I had to stop myself from laughing at the sock suspenders that was attached to his socks and shirt to keep the shirt from rising out of the pants.

I tucked the shirt in on the side seams to give

him a better feel. I pinned it then told him to pull his pants back up to see how it felt.

"That feels much better. You said you can alter them now?"

"Yes. It'll take maybe a half an hour or so."

"Great. I'll wait."

"Okay, I'll do them all. Make yourself comfortable." I took all three of Steven's shirts and went into the small sewing room that was adjacent to my office.

I made the alterations and returned to the office to find a completely naked Steven. "Oh, excuse me." I covered my eyes. I didn't know why that was my first reaction. Maybe it was his sexy physique or his caramel-colored skin or maybe the shock that he was completely naked. Then again, it could've been his long, beautiful dick that pointed in my direction.

"What? You don't like what you see? Come here."

I moved slowly towards him as he stood erect in every sense of the word. When I got up on him, I could feel his breath. It was intoxicating. I stepped back to get a better look. His body was beautiful. And his dick, with its milk chocolate color and perfect curve, had me wanting to see how many licks it would take to get to the center. I stared at it for a moment before taking off my clothes. Good thing I wore something sexy. I fingered Steven to come to me as I walked backwards toward the couch.

"What will make you happy, Jalisa?"

"Touch me here." I directed his hand to my "honeypot."

He slowly teased my clit with one hand and

stroked his long shaft with the other. Watching him go up and down on it was making me hot. He looked at me then at his dick and knew from the wetness of my pussy and the size of my clit that I was aroused. "Like this?"

"Yes." I leaned all the way back and spread my legs so that he would have full access. I gyrated my hips to the movements of his hands.

"May I pleasure you, Jalisa?"

That's a dumb-ass question. "Yes."

With that, Steve positioned me so that I was upside down on the couch, my legs were wide open, while my head hung over the edge of the couch. He stepped over me so that my head was between his legs and I could see his pot of gold. He lowered his head between my legs. The warmth from his tongue sent chills throughout my entire body. Slowly, he twisted his tongue around my clit then he hardened it and stuck it into my pussy. With measured strokes, Steven tasted every inch of me.

"Steven, damn! I never—"

He shut me up when he stuck his finger in my ass. "Am I pleasuring you?"

Quinton had never done that.

"Yes, Steven." My confirmation sent him into a sexual rave that made me orgasm back to back. That double-penetration definitely made me happy.

"Um . . . you taste good." He licked my butter off his lips, and my pussy pulsated from the magic he was doing with his tongue.

Moments later I lifted my head up then swung my body around so that I was sitting on the couch.

"How do you feel?" Steven began to put his clothes back on.

"What are you doing?"

"What do you mean what am I doing?"

"You're putting on your clothes and you haven't cum yet."

"Jalisa, I was pleasuring you; this wasn't about me."

"Yeah, but—"

"Shhhhh. Next time, I promise."

" 'Next time'? There's going to be a next time?"

"Do you want there to be a next time?"

"I want some dick now, if you really want to know the truth."

"Do tell. How bad?"

I took his question as a dare. I walked over to him. "I don't want it bad, I want it good. I want it real good."

"So take it then."

With that, I took his clothes back off. I got on my knees and softly kissed the head of his semi-hard chocolate stick. In my mind, it even tasted like chocolate. I flicked my tongue along the edges of it, wetting it completely. With one of my hands I pumped his stick as I sucked him, while I teased my pussy with the other.

Steven took my head and guided me, making me take him deeper into my mouth.

"Your dick tastes so good, I want to ride it."

"Keep sucking it. You're making me hard as hell, Jalisa."

The slurping sounds that came from me sucking the shit out of his dick clearly had Steven and his dick wanting to scream.

"Jalisa, how could he not want to be inside of you?" he asked, knowing full well he had to wait until I was finished with him before he got an answer.

His question made me move my hips more. The juices from my pussy were oozing down my leg.

"Let me give you some of this." He helped me to stand up.

He didn't have to ask me twice. Shoot, one set of lips was still open because I wanted to taste him some more; the other set was open because my clit was thick as hell.

He led me to my desk and lifted me up so that my ass was in the air as I planted my arms on the desk for support. At first he entered me slowly, sticking the head in, taking it out, then going deeper with every stroke.

"Just fuck me, Steven, I don't want to be teased."

With that, he entered me and fucked me relentlessly. His stroke was on point like a decimal. I closed my eyes and saw black and blue. I just knew, when he was done, that's what my pussy would be.

"Oh *(pump)* Steven, *(pump, pump, pump)* this feels, sooo *(pump)* oooo *(pump, pump, pump)* g-goooooooood." I lost count of his movements as I drifted off into ecstasy. Steven was giving me the goods, and I took it like it was mine. I pushed, he pulled, and we were getting it in.

"Move up a little." He put my legs on the desk in a frog-like position and it was open season on my ass. "Can I please you there?" He softly licked my asshole.

Croak. I had to think about that one. Fingers are one thing; a dick as big and thick as his was another.

He sucked me until I was wet then asked me again, "Jalisa, is this what friends are for?"

"Yes, and right now you're my best buddy in the whole wide world, take it."

Life was something. I went from getting no sex to getting sexed in every conceivable orifice on my body, all within twenty-four hours.

Chapter 15

Valen

When I called the phone number listed in the ad, I was nervous. Well, I was angry and full of anxiety from Roger's nonsense. I never thought our marriage was so weak. People looked at us and thought we were so well put together. He looked sharp in his uniforms, and I shined in my name-brand suits as I held onto his arms.

My body looked worn, although it hadn't been touched in months. Every day when I looked into the mirror, something changed about the way my eyes were set. My mouth was slightly puckered, my jaws hurt from grinding my teeth, and there seemed to be a permanent crease between my eyebrows. In addition, my hairline was receding by my temples and I could see my cheeks sagging.

Hearing Lyda and Jalisa tell me what they'd seen Roger doing shocked me. I was beyond upset,

I was mortified. He'd stooped to an all-time low. There was absolutely nothing else that he could say or do to me that would make me feel any security in my sorry excuse of a marriage.

As I sat in the reception area of the escort service, I pulled out my compact to make sure I had no oil spots on my face. The room was empty, with the exception of one woman who sat across from me and a man who sat in the corner. He was quite handsome, dressed in a pair of designer jeans, white Air Force One's, and a baseball hat. Jewelry that glistened with his every move hung from his neck. I guess that was what they call the thugged-out look. The woman on the other hand was quite trashy. Her fuchsia lipstick clashed with the lime-green tank dress that was skin tight. Her faux fur shoulder wrap looked like it had been dried on full blast. It was clumpy and had burn spots throughout. Her hair was all done up with gel and what I assumed was a hairpiece. The edges of her hairline were sprinkled with gray tentacles, and the ponytail that stuck out from the back of it was ebony black and straight as a pencil. *What the hell am I doing here?*

The room was neatly organized. Chairs lined the walls three-quarters of the way, and a table with pencils and questionnaires sat on the other wall.

After waiting about a half an hour, a woman came out and greeted us. "Welcome. This is your first step to personal freedom and growth. If you haven't already filled out a questionnaire, please do so. Please knock on the door when you're finished." With that, she left us to complete the paperwork.

I walked over and picked up a clipboard. It was a relatively short questionnaire; it consisted of five questions: Are you married? Would you be willing to escort on overnight trips? Do you prefer men, women, or either? Do you prefer weekdays or weekends? (And last but not least.) If you could charge someone any amount of money to spend time with you, how much would that amount be?

"These are weird questions," I whispered to myself and began to answer them. When I was done, I walked up to the door that separated us and the woman and gently knocked.

"Ah, yes," the woman chimed as she opened the door and invited me in.

What a difference in the room I stepped into and the waiting room. Scented candles were placed throughout, giving it an aura of intimacy. This one had fresh cut flowers, a CD playing of birds and tropical rainstorms, a few platters of cold cuts, vegetables, and dips, and fresh lemonade and orange juice.

"This is really nice."

"Thank you, and welcome."

"Thanks," I said, admiring the old Victorian furniture.

"Have a seat." The woman led me to a sitting area. "So what brings you here?" She opened a stenograph pad and began to write.

"Well, I think I was just answering an ad in the paper. I'm not sure exactly why I'm here, but here I am," I said with a sassy twist of my neck. I was out of my element. Being an escort was way out of my league of things that I should be doing to get Roger's attention.

"Okay. Are you familiar with what it is we do here?"

"The ad said dates needed for companionship. Was the ad wrong? Did I misunderstand something?"

"No, I think you got the idea of it, but I can elaborate if you need me to. The service that we offer is one of convenience. I can see that you are a little nervous, and that's normal for first-timers. Trust me, when you get the hang of it, it'll come naturally.

"Our customer base ranges from superior court judges to your local garbage man. So even though you have the last say in choosing your date, you will get requests from an array of individuals. If you have any prejudices, you may want to tell them to me now. However, money is money, no matter where it comes from."

" 'Money'?"

"Yes, money. You will get paid to go out on dates with these individuals. And in some cases you may be escorting women to various functions and charity events. Most times, you can name your price, but we also have a pricing guideline to assist you in pricing appropriately."

"I was under the impression that this was more of a pastime."

"You can consider it anything you wish. Just know that whatever you wish to see it as, you will get paid in the process. You will have to claim this income on your taxes, so I like to tell my girls, 'Get as much money as you can in cash.' "

"How do I choose, or does someone choose me?"

"The basic questionnaire that you completed will give me an idea of how flexible you are. See, the people who come to me are married and single. Sometimes they don't want to bring their spouses to certain events because it's an ego thing; they want to further impress whomever they're trying to impress. Others do it with the hopes that they will meet someone whom they feel comfortable with and eventually develop a relationship where they go away together or just have an understanding."

"What kind of understanding?" I asked. I didn't even know her name, and she was talking to me like we'd known each other longer than the fifteen minutes that I'd been there. "Excuse me, what is your name?"

"Oh my dear, I'm sorry. My name is Penelope."

"Well, it's nice to meet you, Penelope. Please continue."

"If you're out and having a good time, things may or may not go to another level. Dinner and drinks may turn into an orgy of some sort."

"You'll have to excuse me, but what is an orgy?"

"Okay, listen . . . you're new, and it may not even go there; we'll cross that bridge when we get to it. When do you think you want to get started?"

"Let me think about, and I'll get back to you. I just need to absorb what you've already told me."

"I think that's a great idea. Here's my card and call me anytime."

"Thank you." I walked past the table with the

cold cuts on it, picked up a few slices of turkey and cheese and left. I was kind of excited at the notion of being admired by other men. This was going to be a new beginning for me.

Chapter 16

Lyda

Dr. Soreno didn't seem concerned with anything about my "area," so I was thinking that Anthony was just upset because of what I said to him about his broken dick.

On my way home, I stopped by Rick's liquor store. I grabbed a bottle of Tequila Rose. When I got up to the counter to pay for it, a guy was buying lottery tickets in abundance. "Someone's feeling lucky today." I looked at all of the tickets spread out in front of him.

"Yes, this must be my lucky day, you are beautiful."

"Thank you." I laughed.

He extended his hand. "My name is Terry."

"I'm Lyda," I said as I handed the cashier a twenty.

"I see you like 'the Rose.'"

"Yes, I do. I tried it for the first time a few weeks ago and have been hooked ever since."

"Do you have a dollar?"

"A dollar? Yeah." I handed him a dollar. "If you win, you owe me dinner."

"Okay. Write your phone number down." He ripped off piece of my brown bag and grabbed a pen from the register.

I wrote my number down and took his, grabbed my bag, and was out. *That was a nice encounter.*

When I got home, I immediately reached for a glass and filled it with ice. I poured a drink and sat down to open the bills. Everything was due, the rent, cable, my cell phone, and the house phone. The phone bill for the house looked rather thick. When I opened it and saw the balance of $337.52, I went bonkers. Ballistic. Lost my gotdam mind. "What the fuck!" I opened the detailed pages and saw rows and rows of 900 numbers, tons of them. "I can't believe this shit."

I called Anthony.

"Hello."

"You punk-ass motherfucker! I'm sitting here looking at the house phone bill and there's nothing but 900 numbers on it. You'll play me out like that? I let you stay here rent-free, with no responsibilities, and you go and run my phone bill up to $300? What kind of mess is that?"

"I don't know what you're talking about; I didn't run up your phone bill."

"Yeah, okay. You ain't shit. No wonder you can't stay hard for more than three minutes you jerk off to perfect strangers who talk dirty to your stupid ass and get your money, or *my* money. You know what, you better come off with the loot to pay this shit. Who else could it've been, Anthony?"

"Lyda—"

"I want my money, Anthony. This is really fucked up. Where am I supposed to get the money to pay this? I have other bills due, Anthony!"

"I'll get you the money. But can I come over so we can talk about this and what I said to you the other day?"

"There's nothing to talk about, Anthony. You can't, or now I can say don't, want to satisfy me because you're more interested in having phone sex. You motherfuckers never cease to amaze me."

"I know it was wrong, but it's not you. I'm sorry for saying what I said."

I tossed the phone bill to the side and opened my rent statement. *Thank God he can't mess that up.*

Anthony was still talking as I opened my cell phone bill.

I went over on the minutes and that added another $45.00 to the bill. Tossed that mess to the side too. The cable bill was next. I opened it, and my jaw hit the floor. "I'm going to kill you." In addition to my regular bill, there were charges for movies ordered.

"What? Kill me?"

"The cable bill, you ordered movies?"

He hesitated. "No."

"Fuck you, Anthony! Goodbye!" I hung up the phone.

Where did I give him the impression that he could take advantage of me like that? I allowed him in my home with his no-stroke-having ass, and all he did was create more bills for me.

See, Boyfriend, he wasn't the brightest crayon in the box, but he would never do something like this to me, didn't require too much attention and always had cash. Whenever I let him stay over a few nights, he always bought dinner and groceries. And when he left, he would slide me a few dollars for my pocket.

My money wasn't all that right either. I'd saved up enough and balanced my monthly bills to the cent, and these unexpected overages were going to break the little bank I'd saved up.

The doorbell rang. I peeked through the peephole. I didn't want to answer the door, but my nosy neighbor, Charletta, wouldn't give up if I didn't. If she saw my car, she wouldn't stop knocking until I answered the door. I sighed as I let her in.

"Hey, girl, what's up?"

"Nothing. That fool, Anthony, went and ran up my bills."

"Doing what? And what's the big deal, doesn't he have money to cover those bills?"

"I don't know. They're my bills nonetheless and have to be paid whether he gives me money or not."

"Well, how much do you need? I can help you."

"I can't ask you to do that, girl, but thank you."

"Please . . . that's what friends are for."

I didn't exactly consider Charletta a friend. She was a neighbor that I said hi to whenever I saw her, and that was it. She had two children of her own that she had to take care of, and I must say, she did a great job with them. They were very well-mannered and were always dressed nice, even if they didn't always wear the brand-name gear and have the newest Air Jordan's.

Charletta was recently divorced from her husband. I swear, some men were born with the brand "Made in Assholeland." He did her so wrong. Not only did he have an affair with the mail lady, but he also had three children with her right under Charletta's nose.

During the holidays, Charletta would give her a little something for making sure that her mail was delivered promptly and on time. She even went as far as to buy her things for her birthday and invited her to a few functions at her house. She had no idea that, all the while, Ms. Mail Lady was sleeping with her husband.

I had to give the mail lady her props, she never led on to Charletta that she was with her husband, even when she'd seen him act affectionate towards Charletta.

Anyhow, since he'd been gone, she'd been working overtime at her job. She got home around seven and then had to cook dinner and make sure the kids did their homework. When I saw that she was getting uptight or aggravated, I offered to go over there and get the kids ready for the next day, put a load or two of laundry in for her. Anything to make her day a little easier.

*　*　*

"Thanks, Charletta. If I need you I'll let you know."

"Okay. What are you doing this evening?"

"Nothing. I got my bottle of Tequila Rose, and I plan on having a drink or two. You're welcome to stay and join me."

After Charletta got the kids and set them up with a movie in my bedroom, we talked about everything under the sun and drank until we were both feeling no pain. I really enjoyed my conversation with her.

Chapter 17

Jalisa

When Quinton came home, I was stretched out on the couch, drinking a glass of wine. I stopped at TJ Maxx and bought a new nightgown and matching robe to lounge around in. It was white with soft pink flowers embroidered on it. The robe was the same but had white feathers on the cuffs.

I was so relaxed. My pussy was still dripping wet from the day's activities, and I had to sit on the side of my butt because it felt like Steven was still in there.

He was the perfect gentleman. Not once did he push me to do anything that I didn't want to do. What happened earlier was of my own free will, and I loved every minute of it. *I will definitely be calling Steven when I need a friend.*

"Hello." Quinton's tone was unusually happy.

"Hi," I said with apprehension.

"How was your day?"

I had a fuck-filled day, thank you. "Good. And yours?"

"It was okay. Today was a good day. The manager that I was training handled the restaurant all alone." He went into the kitchen and grabbed a beer.

Quinton came and sat in the chair opposite me.

His behavior was strange to me, but I didn't say anything. I was still feeling myself. I looked over my wineglass as I took a sip.

He opened his beer, took a long swig, then let out a soft burp. "Jalisa, do you think that one person can fulfill the needs and wants of another?"

"What do you mean?"

"Do you think that you have everything you want in me and me alone?"

"I did, but you tell me every day that I don't. Your actions tell me that you don't want to be my everything. I don't necessarily believe that's the way of the world, but I do believe that it's a person's own thinking. Why?"

"Just asking. You seem really unhappy with me at times and unappreciative of what I'm trying to do."

"Well, are you trying to split us up? Because with the way you've been and the way you act when I try to talk to you, you're making me not want to even talk to you about things that are bothering me. All you do is turn the tables around to make it look like I'm being selfish, and you never take any responsibility."

"It is selfish of you to kick my back in every night because I don't come home and put in another eight hours of working *you*. I'm a man, not a machine. So, yes, I do think you're selfish, and excuse me for getting aggravated with you after coming home from a long and tiring day at the restaurant. It gets old after a while, Jalisa."

"Oh and that's when I have to do me?"

"You completely misunderstood what I was saying, which is another bad character flaw of yours."

"If I make you so miserable, why don't you divorce me?"

"You don't make me miserable, you make yourself miserable, and you take it out on me. Maybe you need to be involved in more self-gratifying things, instead of needles and thread. Maybe you're the one putting too many hours in on the job and need more playtime, have you ever thought of that?"

"Not until you just said something. And you know what, I agree with you. I should do more things that bring me more satisfaction, instead of always trying to satisfy everyone else. Yes, I think maybe that's what I need to do, me."

He shot me a confused look. "So you understand where I'm coming from?"

"Um hum," I mumbled. "Exactly."

Chapter 18

Jalisa

I called Lyda and Valen and invited them to lunch. I was ready to play.

"Girl, we never come here. Quinton is going to know that something's up."

"Lyda, there's nothing up. Why can't we have lunch here?"

"Because we never do," Valen said.

"Yeah, well there's a first time for everything."

We pulled into the parking lot. It was brunch time, and the restaurant looked like it was packed. As I expected, Darrell was there at the entrance greeting customers, dressed in his uniform and looking real good.

"Look, y'all."

Lyda and Valen looked over and past Darrell. "What are we looking at?"

I pointed to him.

"Okay, and . . . ? Lyda laughed. "He's marking off tables."

I gave them a wink and approached him. "How you doing, Darrell?" I touched his hand.

"Oh, hi. How are you?" He seemed pleasantly surprised.

"I'm good. I was wondering if you had a table for me and my girlfriends. One that's away from the crowd so we may have a little privacy."

"We're crowded this afternoon, as you can see, but give me a few minutes. Let me see what we have in the back."

"Okay. Thank you." I turned to face Lyda and Valen. "What?" I shrugged my shoulders.

"You ought to be ashamed of yourself. You need your ass beat, trying to pick up that teenager." Lyda laughed.

"I'm not trying to pick him up, and he's not a teenager."

"Um hum, looks like it to me." Valen was cracking up.

"For your information, I'm not trying to pick him up, I'm trying to put it down, girl." I did the "hump" dance.

"Oh, I know that shit is right." Lyda started to dance too.

"You two are some fools."

Darrell came back and grabbed three menus. "Right this way, please."

We followed him.

"Look at that tight ass. Young, fresh, tight ass, couldn't ask for anything else."

"Now what do you plan on doing with that? And

how are you going to pull that one off when he works for Quinton?" Lyda was still laughing.

"I'm going to do me. We can do whatever his little sexy ass wants to do."

"Shhhh. You're loud."

"I know, Valen; I want him to hear me."

Darrell turned to us like he'd heard what we said. "Is this table okay?"

"It's perfect, Darrell. Thank you." I gave him a wink.

"Do you need to see a drink menu, or would you rather go to the bar?"

"We'll go to the bar, sweetheart."

"Okay. Your server will be right with you."

We walked over to the bar and ordered our drinks. The place was really happening even at lunchtime. There was a live band playing, and people were really having a nice time. We sat at the bar for the first round then took the second back to our table.

"This is really nice. Quinton is doing the damn thing," Lyda said.

"Yeah, he is. I can't believe that you've never been to your own husband's restaurant."

"I know, Valen. I said that to him the other day. I told him that I'll be supporting him more. But, wait, let me tell you about what he said to me last night. He said that no one person can be everything to another."

"No, the fuck, he didn't," Lyda snapped. "He wasn't serious."

"Yes, he did, and yes he was."

"What man in their right mind would say that to his wife?"

"It gets better. The other day when we were talking, he told me to do me, that if I need something that he's not offering, I need to go and find someone who will give it to me."

"Wait, what was the conversation about?"

"I told him that I needed more passion and that he needed to be more in tune with our relationship and what it's lacking."

"And so he tells you to get that from someone else?"

"Yes, that's what I got from it. And when he said that mess about one person not being able to completely satisfy the other, I mean, what else am I supposed to think? I'm tired of trying to let him know how I feel and him not hearing me. He doesn't even kiss me, what does that say? Isn't kissing the most intimate part of showing someone that you love them?"

"Yes. I need that. I haven't had it, but I do need it," Valen said.

"Umph, not me. All I need is the dick. And if cutie pie don't work out for you, send his young butt right over to me."

I laughed. "Shut up, Lyda."

By the time we got our food and finished it, we were well into our fourth drink. We laughed about Lyda's phone and cable bill and Roger's bullet-ridden blow up doll. We all felt the stresses of our lives float away with our laughter as we enjoyed each other's company.

"We have definitely got to do this again," Valen slurred.

"I'm not going to have any extra money, so you guys can bring me a doggy bag."

"Lyda, please . . . you know we got you. We eat, you eat. We girls, remember?"

We ate as much as we could. I couldn't finish my food, so I had it wrapped up. "Where are you guys going?" I asked. "I'm going home and lay down."

"I'm going to try and find me some dick," Lyda said.

Then Valen reminded us, "I have to make a run into my new womanhood."

Chapter 19

Valen

I sat in my car for a moment and held the card that Penelope had given me. When I'd called and told her that I wanted to go forward, she sounded so delighted. I still wasn't sure why I was there or what was going to come out of it, but I felt like I needed to do this. Hell, I needed to do something because my self-esteem was at rock bottom.

This time, the reception area was busy. I gave my name, and Penelope came right out.

"I'm so glad you decided to come. I think you'll be surprised at what you can do here."

"I know I sound ignorant, but where do I begin?"

"Anywhere you want. If you want to go on a very casual outing, we have clients for that. If you want to be pampered, go to dinner and be treated like a lady, we have clients for that as well. And if you want to go way out the box, well, when you're ready, we have clients for that too."

"No. Nothing too much at first."

"Very well. Let me pull up my database."

While Penelope found my "match," I looked around her office. There were tons of pictures of her with different men. Some were old, and some were young enough to be her son.

Penelope wasn't a bad-looking woman. Her caramel complexion and red freckles told me that she was mixed with something. Her brassy hair was in a short curly Afro style. She had green eyes, voluptuous breasts, an ample waist, long legs, and the prettiest feet I'd ever seen. The color on her toes was a shimmering sheer white, and she had stark white flowers painted on her two big toes.

"Who are all of these different men in all of these pictures?"

She chuckled. "Honey, I've had my business for a long time now. Those are a few of the men who I've become very close with."

"Were any of them ever your client?"

"They all started of as clients, but then things changed. That was husband number one, Michael. We lasted all of three years. He tried to change me, and I just wasn't having that." She pointed to the picture hoisted above a tiny fireplace on the far wall.

"That was husband number two," She pointed to the picture that sat on one of her end tables, "Brad. His obsession for women of color didn't allow him to be with just me. In this business, you call the shots. They're to be with you and only you.

It's up to them to keep it under wraps if they're with other women. Don't accept a liar; a liar is a thief and a cheat, they're all one and the same."

"Wow, you've really lived, huh?"

"Yes, I have. If I don't live for myself, who's gonna live for me? I was married to a man before I got into the business. I believe that his sole purpose for being born was to make my life miserable. All he did was come home every day and beat my ass. He told me I wasn't shit and would never be shit without him. He brainwashed me into believing I was nothing.

"One day it hit me, if I allow myself to be put down, beaten, and hated, I couldn't love myself at all. I just got out of bed one day and left. And you know what, we only have one thing that keeps us in charge."

"What's that?"

"The pussy! There are a few dudes, probably thousands, if you want to get technical, who don't appreciate it. The essence of it can drive a man wild without ever tasting it or smelling it. And you can wear it too, did you know that?"

" 'Wear' my pussy? I don't get it."

"Say you're at a party, you have on your sexy dress, your hair is done, you know, you look good, right. How you walk, talk, do your hands, throw your hair, and use your lips will determine whether or not you hold a man's mind captive. Men are visual creatures, and if you do all of those things right, they'll visualize being inside of you, tasting you, feeling your heat. Girl, I'm telling you, it got me rich."

"How did you get stronger mentally? I mean

after fifteen years of being in an abusive relationship, you must've been pretty tired."

"I didn't have time to be tired. Life was passing
me by. I'd wasted enough time. I needed to be
strong right then, not a day later."

I was intrigued by Penelope's story. I too was
tired, and Roger and I hadn't been married that
long. *If I stay for fifteen years, I'll be diminished; he will
break me down to nothing. I can't allow him to do that.*

"Okay. I looked at my list of possible clients.
There were a few who wanted basic companionship. Shall I send an ice-breaker to them on your
behalf?"

"What's an 'ice-breaker'?"

"It's an email introducing our newest escort. I'll
have to take your picture and a little bit more information so that they can have some idea of what
you're about."

"I didn't bring a picture with me; I didn't know
I would need one."

"Not to worry, honeydew. I can take your picture here. We're going to get you some playtime.
All you have to do is say that you're ready."

I was nervous and was excited at the same time.
The idea of any man being remotely turned on be-
cause of anything about me made me smile inside.
"I'm ready."

Penelope didn't waste any time getting her digi-
tal camera out and taking my picture.

Since I was dressed modestly, she loaned me a
low-cut blouse that showed a little bit of skin. We
played with my hair a little bit so that I looked ad-
venturous. Then we uploaded my picture and
worked on my profile.

Two hours later, I was set up in her database. Once she clicked the *send* button, everyone in her address book would get an e-mail introducing me and inviting them to call me anytime.

I left the office feeling like a new person. The nervousness had gone away once the e-mail was sent. There was no turning back now.

As I drove home, my eyes welled up. Part of me felt like I'd been minimized by what I was about to do, but the other part of me felt like it was about time that I started to take care of me. I began to cry because I didn't know why Roger treated me the way he did. *He really must not like me.* "Well, what's done is done."

I got out of my car and went into the house.

Roger was sitting at his computer.

I walked past him and into the kitchen. I poured myself a glass of Scotch, which I never drank, and sat at the dining room table. I could hear the clicking of the keys on Roger's keyboard.

"Damn recruits!" he yelled. "Always want time for this girl or that girl, useless."

I shook my head in disbelief and wondered if he treated everyone with the same little respect he treated me. "I'm going to lay down." I walked back past him and to my bedroom.

A few minutes later, I was taking off my clothes when he came up from behind me. "You didn't take our little argument seriously, did you?"

He made my skin crawl. I didn't answer. I just stood there, motion-and emotionless.

"Bend over." He rubbed his semi-hard penis on my back. Normally, he would have to ramble off a bunch of vulgarities to get turned on.

I wasn't sure what his problem was, but he was getting harder from just rubbing on me as I stood there. "Not now, Roger, I'm tired."

"You know I don't go for that nonsense. We're going to do this." He continued to rub up against me.

I turned and faced him. "Roger, you will not have sex with me tonight. I can answer your question for you now, no, I'm not cumming. I haven't cum while having sex with you, not once. I've faked every funky, nasty moment that I've been with you. There is nothing that I enjoy about being with you. All you've ever done was beat me down and tried your damnedest to keep me there."

He took a few steps back.

"Do us both a favor, go get another blow up doll, that will be the only piece of ass you'll be getting up in here." I walked into the bathroom and closed the door behind me.

Chapter 20

Jalisa

I dropped Valen and Lyda off and came back to the restaurant. Darrell was still at the front desk. I stood back and watched him handle the customers waiting to be seated. When I saw that he had a free moment, I softly whistled to get his attention. "Psssst, Darrell."

He looked up.

"When do you get a break?"

"In about a half an hour. Why?"

"I was hoping we could go somewhere and talk."

"Talk about what?"

"Just come outside when you go on break."

"Okay."

While I waited I called Lyda and Valen and told them what I was about to do.

"How are you going to rob the cradle like that?" Valen asked.

"I'm not, I just want to see where his head is; maybe he's attracted to me too."

"I don't know. He's pretty young-looking."

"Lyda, I thought you would be backing a sister on this."

"Hey, I feel you, but you're gonna end up worse than me. What in the hell are you going to do with a boy his age?"

"I wouldn't knock it until I tried it," Valen said.

"What . . . you think I should try and get me some?"

"All I'm saying is that sometimes it's like that. How old are we? We have husbands and a boyfriend who can't please us. I don't see anything wrong with it, Jalisa. In the words of Quinton, 'Do you.'"

That's all I needed, validation from my girlfriends. I was there already, but it helped to know that they had my back. No matter what, they were always down for whatever I wanted to do, and I was the same way with them.

Just as Darrell said, he was outside in half an hour. He had taken off his uniform. When he got in the car, I got a little bit nervous.

"So what's up?"

"Nothing. I just wanted to spend a little time with you."

"Really? Why?"

"To be honest, Darrell, I think you're very attractive. I know you work for my husband, and I would completely understand if you jumped out of the car and ran for your life." I laughed, but he didn't.

Before I could say another word, he reached over and grabbed me by the back of the head. He kissed me then playfully slipped me his tongue.

I pretended to be shocked. "Whoa!"

"What? I know you feeling me, don't fight it, baby."

I looked at him. "How old are you, Darrell?"

"Twenty."

"You're twenty years old? I'm in my late twenties. Do you think you would have a problem with that? Or better yet, do you have a problem with the fact that I'm married to Quinton?"

"No, not really. He's just my boss; he's not my dawg or nothing like that. Hey, I know how it goes, dude ain't hitting you off like he should be, right?"

"Why do you assume that?"

"Well, for one, he's always working, he's here at the restaurant all of the time, and second, he never jokes around with us about sex; he's so corny. But anyway, you are fine."

I laughed. I shouldn't have been surprised at his arrogance. Here I was, a grown-ass woman, trying to get with a young boy who's not even of drinking age. "Thank you. So when can we spend some real time together? Maybe we can go and get something to eat."

"Ain't no time like the present. I'm off. I told Quinton that I had a family emergency."

"How did you know why I wanted to see you?"

"Come on now, I read right through you. So where would you like to go."

*   *   *

The hotel that he chose wasn't the greatest, but it served the purpose. Before we could even get into the room, Darrell had his hands all over me.

I was half undressed and wanted to freshen up before anything went down. I tried to go into the bathroom, but he came right behind and put me up on the sink. He tore open a condom, rolled it on his dick, and wasted no time in setting it off.

I pulled my panties to the side and welcomed Darrell to my world.

His movements were sharp and full of force.

My back was pressed up against the faucet, which was grinding on my bone. I held onto the edge of the sink as he pinned my legs open as much as he could. My head kept banging against the mirror, and I was sliding off the sink. "Let's go to the bed." I was panting.

He picked me up and carried me over to the bed.

My legs were still wrapped around him. I wasn't trying to let his dick slip out. Yes, it was that good.

"How you like this?"

"It's good. Harder, baby."

He gave me that twenty-year-old dick, and I loved the shit out of it. Darrell flipped me over and took it doggie-style. He held onto my ass so tight when he went in and out, there was hardly any space between my ass and his pelvic area. He was talking mad shit. "Damn! Mr. Quinton missing out on this here."

I couldn't even respond. My insides were getting tossed out of this world. Chills were going up and down my back as he lay his pipe down. I reached under and gently tickled his balls.

Darrell double-timed his stroke, knocking my forehead into the headboard. "I'm sorry, but when you touched me, it drove me crazy. This pussy is so good. Too bad for Mr. Quinton."

I wasn't paying any mind to Darrell. I didn't want to say anything to him that would throw him off of the path of claiming the title of "the best pussy-pounder of the year."

When our time spent together was over, I took Darrell back to the restaurant. "Do you need a ride home?"

"Nah, I got my ride in the back. Come here."

I leaned over, and Darrell gave me a kiss on the lips. "Thank you."

"For what?" I asked.

"Fo' dat ass!"

I busted out laughing. "See you later, Darrell."

He got out of the car, and I waited to make sure he got off okay. He pulled off in an Infinity truck. *That's sexy.*

He pulled up in front of me. "Let me know when I can give you some more of this dick."

"Oh, I definitely want some more." I tooted my horn and carried my ass home.

Chapter 21

Lyda

Anthony stood in the doorway. I really didn't want to let him in, but if it meant that I was going to get my money, I could tolerate him for a little while. "Come in, Anthony."

"Lyda, look, I know you think I was the one calling the 900 numbers, but I'm telling you, it wasn't me; I wouldn't do that. I know it bothers you that I cum too quickly or not at all, but I told you what the problem was."

"Do I look like a jackass to you? Right now, all I'm trying to hear is you going in your pocket and peeling off $1,600 to pay these bills. If you're not doing that, there's no reason for you to be here. And for the record, I'm good in that area. Just a little bacteria build up."

"Well, I need to talk to you about the money. I don't have the full amount right now, but if you let me make payments, I could pay you off in a few months."

" 'Payments'? What do I look like to you? The bills won't and can't wait. I want my money, and I want it now, Anthony. I'm really not trying to get ignorant with you, but I will, *bel'e dat*!"

"You'll get your money, baby. Just let me come back."

"Ah, NO! Bye." I opened the door for him to leave and just as I was closing it, Boyfriend pulled up. His timing couldn't be better. " 's up, Boyfriend? I was going to call you back, but I got busy. Come on in."

Anthony shot me a look. He greeted Boyfriend as he was coming up to the door. "How you doing? I'm Anthony."

"A'ight," Boyfriend said in his ignorant-ass way.

I was cracking up. "Hey, baby. I missed you."

Anthony looked at me like, *Bitch, oh no, you didn't.*

"I missed you too."

"I know. Can I get you something to eat?" I closed the door in Anthony's face, and Boyfriend and I went inside.

"Damn, baby, this is good."

I'd made some salmon cakes and grits. "Yeah, I'm glad you like it."

"A'ight. You need anything?"

"Well, funny you should ask. That dude you just saw, well, he's been over here a few times and he ran up both my cable and phone bill. I don't have the money with me not working and all to cover it all the way. So, yes, if you could slide me a little something-something, I'd really appreciate it."

"Yeah. How much?"

I knew what that meant, and you know what, I was so down for it. I took Boyfriend by the hand and led him into the bedroom.

He turned me around and ripped my clothes off. He knew I liked that rough shit. Then he bent me over and began to lick me from the top of my crack all the way down to my clit. He lifted me so that my ass was in the air and was tonguing me down, tossing my salad. It was all of that. Boyfriend flipped me over and began to rub up and down his shaft. He was one fine-ass chocolate brother, and his dick was so smooth. My juice had it so wet, I could hear him going up and down on it. That shit turned me on.

I opened my legs and gave him a show. My lips were swollen from anticipation and from what he just did to them. I spread them so that my clit stuck out and went to work. I moved my hips in a rhythm that made him come closer to me.

He stood between my legs as I worked it. "Damn, baby, you making my dick hard as hell."

"You want it, don't you?"

"Hell yeah, but keep playing with it."

"Okay, baby." I continued to play by licking my own juices off my fingers.

"Oh shit, girl!"

"You my daddy?"

"Your uncle and your cousin too." He kept pumping his dick, which by now was HUGE!

"You about to cum?"

"Not yet. Come taste it."

I quickly sat up and took him into my mouth.

The taste of his butter got me every time. As simple as he was, dude could've had this ass any time, any place.

"Baby," he said softly.

"Yes."

"It's not always going to be like this."

"I know. I'm willing to wait. And I'm sorry for leaving you at DMV. I had a frustrating moment. I said that I'd wait for you and I will."

He kissed me on my head, and we drifted off to sleep.

Chapter 22

Valen

Tonight was my first date with Bobby, a music producer from Northern New Jersey. We decided to meet at Flava's, a Newark nightclub tucked away on East Park Street. Definitely a place to go if you *didn't* want to be seen. When I walked in, it was kind of empty. There was a live band playing downstairs. Recessed lights and decorative sconces lit up the room, and tiered candles were on every table. The bar was located in the back.

As I walked towards it, I looked around hoping I didn't see any familiar faces. How I would explain being in such a place was beyond me, even though the chance of running into someone who knew Roger was slim.

When Bobby and I talked on the phone a few nights earlier, the conversation flowed as if we'd known each other for a long time. I didn't feel any forcefulness in his voice, or anything that made me feel uncomfortable. And though I could use an intense night of passion, I definitely didn't get that he was after sex.

I took a seat at the bar. I thought I was dressed appropriately, but compared to how the other women were dressed, I felt really uncomfortable. I had on a corduroy blazer that was buttoned, flared-collar white shirt that was cut low in the front, a pair of jeans, and my new bronze boots that I'd just picked up at Macy's. To avoid looking like a complete idiot, I unbuttoned my blazer, put my collar up, tossed my hair a little, and adjusted myself so that I had cleavage.

We were supposed to meet at 8:00. Since I hated being late, I decided to get there at 7:30. With half an hour to kill, I ordered a drink. "Can you please run a tab?" I asked the bartender.

"Yes. What would you like to order?"

"I'll have an Absolut and cranberry." I knew damn well I couldn't drink like that, but oh well . . . tonight was a special occasion.

My cell phone rang just as the bartender handed me my drink. "Hello."

"I'm outside."

"Okay. What? You want me to come and get you?"

"Yes, please."

"Okay. I'll be right out." I took a sip of my drink then took a longer one. I was nervous but I really didn't have time for that. Bobby was paying $250 for my company in a last-minute arrangement. Apparently, a deal had gone bad and he just wanted some company. I wasn't sure how I would be able to comfort him, but I was ready for anything.

I got up and walked towards the front of the

club. As I approached a set of stairs that led to the front of the club, a man stood in front of a table, reading the brochures that were scattered on it. I was so nervous, I forgot which way was out. Besides, the alcohol was taking effect. "Is this the way to the front?"

He looked up at me. "Yes," he answered softly.

I kept walking as I took in all of him. He was dressed real cute in his white do-rag, white baseball cap, white leather jacket, faded lap jeans, and Air Force One sneakers. Three white gold necklaces hung from his neck, a microphone with diamonds in the ball of it, a cross with diamonds, and a dog tag surrounded by diamonds. And his earring had to be at least one carat.

I walked past him, went to the front door, and stuck my head out. I didn't recall him telling me what he was going to wear or what kind of car he drove. No one was out there, so I waited a minute more before closing the door and going back to the bar.

"Hi, Valen."

"You—" I laughed; he laughed. He was beautiful. "I didn't expect—"

"I figured. That's why I let you walk up here. I got a kick out of you watching me and trying to figure out who I was." He extended his hand. "Bobby, and it's nice to meet you."

"Valen, I'm so embarrassed."

"Don't be."

His aura was magnetic. I immediately felt comfortable. His lips looked like they were soft. His eyes were scary in one sense, yet hypnotizing. "Shall we go back to the bar and sit?"

"Okay."

We sat in silence. I really didn't know what to say. I mean, here I was married and out with another man. What kind of person did that make me? And he knew I was married. So what kind of person did that make him? I looked over at him.

"What's wrong, Jalisa?"

"Nothing. It's just that this is my first."

"I know. And if you feel uncomfortable at all, we can end the date here. It's all good."

"No, I don't feel uncomfortable. A little nervous, but not uncomfortable." I looked at his necklaces again. "Whose picture is that?"

"That's my grandmother."

"You have nice jewelry."

"Thank you." He looked at my wedding ring. "So do you. Do you want to talk about it?"

Stupid. Just plain stupid. Maybe the fact that I was married would've just slipped his mind if I had taken off my ring. "No, not really. Besides, he isn't much to talk about."

"Okay. Then if you don't mind, I'll tell you about myself."

"No, I don't mind at all."

During our conversation, I learned that those who knew Bobby well called him Haze, or Fatal Haze. It was his rapping name, and according to him, everything he did was fatal and to die for. He rapped on lots of the famous rappers albums and also produced a few of them as well. At the time, he was shopping his latest album, which was a compilation of various R&B songs. He lived in Newark and also had a house in Teaneck. He had no children, was never married, and had two pit bulls, which he loved dearly.

"So you must've traveled around the world, been lots of places, and seen lots of things?"

"Yes, I have."

"And all this time, you haven't found a woman that you wanted to spend time with? You have to do this?"

"There are women everywhere. Most of them were full of shit and lied about everything."

"Have you ever had sex with any of them?"

"Only the ones I dealt with."

"And was it strictly sexual, or were you into them and something just went wrong?"

I ordered another drink. "Join me."

"I'll have what you're having."

By then, I was completely relaxed and feeling the aura that Haze was giving off. His laid-back attitude was a turn-on. I could tell he was a free spirit.

"There was one, she ended up cheating on me and getting pregnant, twice by two different men."

"Wow! I don't have any children."

"Do you think that you and your husband will have any in the future?"

"No."

Silence took over. Maybe it was the look on my face that told him I didn't want to continue the conversation if it was going to be about me and my husband. We sipped our drinks and looked around the club.

"So what do you do for a living?"

"Nothing. I don't work."

"Was that always the case?"

"No. I used to work as a bank teller until my husband wanted me home."

"Home for what?"

"I don't know. At the time I thought it was because he maybe wanted to spend more time with me, but as time went on, I saw that it was just one of his ways of controlling me." I was trying my hardest not to be rude as he pressed. "I'd really rather not talk about it. We're supposed to be having a nice night out and just relaxing. You did pay for that."

"I've already gotten my money's worth, you are beautiful, and I'm enjoying your company."

"Thank you, Bobby, I mean Haze. Can I ask you a question?"

"Sure."

"Are you that fatal?"

"I can be, but I promise to take it easy on you. Now can I ask *you* a question?"

"Okay." Regardless of how much fun I was having being out with Haze, if he asked me anything about Roger, I was going to leave.

"On our next date, do we have to go through the agency?"

" 'Our next date'?"

"Yes. I'd like to see you again."

I smiled and gave him my cell phone number. We ordered another drink.

That evening with Haze put me in touch with my woman, the woman I'd lost when I said, "I do," to Roger.

Chapter 23

Lyda

"Lyda?"

"Yes. Who's calling?"

"This is Terry, the lottery ticket guy."

"Oh! Hi, Terry. Don't tell me you hit for a million dollars." I laughed.

"No, not exactly. I hit for a nice chunk of change, and I think a celebration is in order. Considering you gave me a dollar to play, you are entitled to some of the profits. So what's it going to be?"

"Boy, you need to stop playing."

"I'm not playing. Let me take you to dinner. That's the least I can do."

I thought about it. I did give him a dollar and hadn't been on a date in I don't know how long. Worst case scenario I can get a free meal. "Okay. Where do you want to meet?"

"I'll pick you up. Give me your address."

* * *

When I'd asked Boyfriend for the money to pay the bills that Anthony ran up, I added a few dollars so that I could have a cushion in the bank. I told him the bills came up to $2000. That gave me a little money to play with.

I ran to the mall and went shopping. I came out with four bags, one from Ann Taylor LOFT, one from Parade of Shoes, one from Silver Stadium, and one from Victoria's Secret. I went home and laid out my clothes. I bought a black suit, a beaded off-white camisole, a pair of black strappy shoes, and a few pairs of thong underwear. Not that he would be seeing them, but I had to feel sexy, since I was going out on an official date.

When Terry picked me up, I was floored. He pulled up in a 2005 Dodge Charger, a black on black with chrome accents. He was dressed in a linen suit, had a fresh haircut and trimmed face, and smelled like a pot of gold. In the passenger seat was a dozen roses and a box of chocolate.

"Terry, exactly how much did you get?"

"Baby, none of that matters. All I know is that I made you a promise and I'm here to deliver." He opened the door and I got in.

We drove to the Reef Club, a sushi restaurant on the shore. Inside, there were huge fish tanks with different kinds of tropical fish all against the walls.

It was a predominantly white crowd, but I didn't mind; I was out having a good time on someone else's dime. The waiter led us to a table that had a "reserved" card on it.

"I called and made reservations."

"Oh really? How did you know I would accept your offer for dinner?"

"I knew you would at least want your dollar back, so here it is." He handed me a dollar.

I took it and sat down. "You are quite charming, Terry."

"Thank you. I bet you completely forgot about that day. I told you if I hit I would call you."

He avoided my question before, so I asked it again. "Are you going to tell me how much you won or not?"

"I won over a hundred grand."

"You . . . are . . . lying."

"No, I'm not."

"How many tickets did you play?"

"The number that I hit was from your dollar."

"So what are you saying?"

He reached inside of his jacket. "This is for you."

I stared at the envelope. *He couldn't be serious; that envelope was probably stuffed with "Geoffrey" money.* I turned up my lips and cut my eyes at him. "You're a comedian, I see."

"What! I'm not joking; this is for you. Just take it and open it."

I grabbed the envelope and opened it. If I had to guess, there was at least twenty thousand dollars in there. "How much?" My hands were shaking.

"Twenty-five thousand."

"What?" That called for the hump dance. I got up and did my thing. "*Uh, now*"—hump, hump, hump—"*What, uh, uh, yeah, drop it like it's hot.*"

Terry started cracking up. "You are crazy. My type of girl."

"Terry, man, thank you so much. Oh my got-damn! I can't believe this shit. Whoa!"

"Well, believe it. Trust me, I know the feeling. Let's enjoy dinner."

As soon I got home, I called Jalisa and Valen.

"You are lying."

"Valen, I swear. He was there in the liquor store buying tickets when I walked in. He asked me for a dollar and told me that if he hit, he would give me some of the money."

"How did he know how to find you?" Jalisa asked.

"We exchanged numbers, but I didn't expect him to call. You know, I thought I was giving to some-body's good cause. I still can't believe it, y'all. Anthony ran up my bills and created some good-ass karma for me."

"Girl, that is so great. It's not often that some-one who is worthy of it catches a break." Valen laughed. "So where are we eating?"

"Who paid the taxes on that, Lyda?"

"I don't know. I guess he did."

Jalisa said, "You know anything over $9,999.99 has to be reported to the IRS."

"Well, that money was awarded to him first, and this is just a gift—ain't no bank gonna see this, okay!"

"I know that's right," Valen said. "So, again, where are we eating?"

"McCormick & Schmick's in the city tomorrow. Be ready at five o'clock; I'll make the reservations for seven."

* * *

"Oh my gosh! These coconut shrimp are slam-
min'."

"Lyda, take human bites. Besides, I don't want
you to choke over what I'm about to tell you."

"What, girl? You don't have anything going on."
Jalisa took a bite out of her Ahi tuna appetizer.

"Damn!" Lyda said. "This shit is good."

"I joined an escort service."

Lyda and Jalisa kept eating as if they hadn't
heard a word I said, but I know they heard me because *I* heard me.

"Excuse me—" I tapped on the table with my
fork. "I said that I joined an escort service, and I
went out on my first date the other night." I knew
that would get their attention.

Lyda chewed slowly, while Jalisa held her food
in her mouth. They both kept their heads down
and looked at their plates. I knew they thought the
worst, that I resorted to the grimy life of prostitution but I quickly enlightened them. "This isn't a
prostitution thing, it's an escort service."

"I know what an escort service is," Lyda said
through clenched teeth.

"Valen, you let Roger fuck your mind up."

"It's not what you guys think. I go out with men
who need company, there is no sex. Everything is
recorded at the office, and that's that. I had a really
nice time, and I have another date tonight."

"Okay. And how does 'Warden' Roger feel
about this?" Jalisa asked.

"It was his idea. We got into an argument the

other day. He said that he was going to cut off the money that he gives me on a weekly basis and that I needed to get a job."

"Target or Pier 1 just wasn't an option, huh?"

"Jalisa, I'm not working in anybody's Target or Pier 1. I'm going to live my life. This job will allow me to meet new people, broaden my horizons, and possibly meet someone special, you never know. Don't go knocking what I'm doing when you're doing it but just in a different way."

"I'm not knocking anything. I'm just saying . . . isn't that a little beneath you?"

"No. Having my husband fuck a plastic doll is beneath me. Damn all of that! If nothing else, I will regain my womanhood."

"I ain't mad at you, girl," Lyda said; "just be careful."

"Yeah, there are come crazy people out there."

"I'm good. Thanks y'all!"

Chapter 24

Jalisa

I already had a seat at the bar when Darrell came into work. That day Quinton had gone golfing with Roger. I still don't understand that, but whatever . . . I had other things to do. I made sure I dressed real cute. I wore my cashmere sweater that sat off the shoulder and had a fur-lined collar, my black fitted slacks, and my black gator cowboy boots. My skin was glistening, my lips were shining, and my coochie was wet!

Dressed in regular clothes, he came in through the main entrance. There was someone else with him, but I couldn't see his face. The person working the reservation booth handed him an envelope, and he walked out.

I took a big gulp from my drink, grabbed my purse, and ran out the door behind him. "Darrell, wait," I yelled.

He turned around and walked to me, and the man with him got in the car.

"Hey, baby. How you doing?"

"Good, honey. Are you working today?"

"Actually, no, I'm not. My dad is taking me to get fitted for some dress shirts. He has the hook up, you know."

"Oh really? And who is your dad?"

"Come on and meet him." He took me by the hand and walked me over to his truck.

As we approached, the man on the passenger side of the truck rolled down the window. He sat there in his tailored suit and the shirt that I'd tailored for him. And damn! he was looking fine as hell.

"This is your father?"

"Hi, Jalisa," Steven said.

"Hey, Steven." I didn't know whether to laugh or cry. I looked over at Darrell.

He put his finger up to his mouth. "Shhhh," he mouthed.

I turned back to Steven, who did the same thing. Now I wasn't no dumb chick. Either they had no idea who I was to the other one, or they were playing me out ungodly.

"We're going to get fitted for some shirts. Want to come for the ride?"

I looked at Steven with apprehension. Then I looked at Darrell, who by that time had climbed into the driver's side of the car.

"So do you want to come?" Darrell asked.

"Yes, I do." I hopped in the car.

Steven must've given Darrell directions to my office before they got there.

In fifteen minutes we were up in my office. Darrell was fucking me from behind, while I had Steven's dick in my mouth. I was in heaven. Steven taught Darrell right because he was hemming me up. We'd moved everything off of my desk, pulled the chair out so that Steven could stand there. Darrell had me on my desk in the same frog-like position his father had me in.

"Did you tell him how I liked it?" I managed to say. "He's fucking me good, just like you did."

"Damn, Jalisa, your shit is good. My father told me that you needed some good dick. Well, here it is. Take this shit. You don't ever have to worry about not getting fucked. We got you."

"Jalisa, I told you that anything you need, I can give to you. We're here to please you."

They worked me like a slave in a sex camp. Steven knew how I liked it from before. I wonder if he told his son that he fucked me the other day. Steven didn't strike me as the type to kiss and tell, but I believed I put it on his ass and maybe he couldn't keep it to himself. I wasn't mad at him. Hell, look what his telling got me, two dicks of a feather, fuck together. *Yummy*!

The following morning, Quinton came in the bedroom, where I was having my coffee, and started complaining about how sore he was. "I never realized how out of shape I was."

I sat there and said nothing. *Hell, I could've told you that.*

"Roger really takes this golf thing seriously. He plays almost every day, and he's really good."

I really couldn't give a shit. "That's nice."

"How was your day yesterday?

He never cared how my day went. Why was he asking me then? "It was good. Uneventful."

"That's nice. So when are you coming down to the restaurant?"

I shrugged my shoulders. "I don't know. We'll see."

"Is everything okay? You're being kind of evasive."

"Things couldn't be better."

Chapter 25

Valen

Kevin was a weird one. He was 45 years old, married with no children. He had dreads that were pulled back into a pony tail and wore clear braces. "So?" he asked.

"So what?"

"What's a nice girl like you doing this for?"

"Well, I thought it would be a nice way to meet people; you can never have too many friends."

"You joined an escort service to make friends?" He laughed.

"Yes." I wasn't feeling his line of questioning. Something told me that this date was going to be short-lived.

He shook his head. "See, it's women like you that mess up everything. You're married, why are you out with other men when you have a husband at home? I bet he doesn't know what you're doing right now. He probably thinks you're out buying dinner napkins or having your feet and nails done."

"Kevin, it was nice meeting you this date is over." I got up and proceeded to walk out.

He yelled, "I bet you think you're not a prostitute, but you are."

I couldn't get out of there fast enough.

"You're nothing but a whore. An hour from now I would've been fucking you in the back seat of my car!"

I ran the rest of the way until I was out of the restaurant and down the block. My heart was racing, and I was short of breath not from running, but because I thought he was going to come after me. I panicked. I bent over to catch my breath. I was glad that I'd parked in the parking garage two blocks away and that he didn't know that. I slowed down and began to walk the rest of the way. I buttoned my coat because it was a little cold outside.

As I approached the entrance to the parking garage, I saw the AAA man towing a car that had blocked the driveway entrance.

"Hey there," I said. "Remember me?" Boy, was I glad to see him.

He looked up and smiled.

"Yes, I do. How are you?"

"I'm good. Was just having dinner with a friend. What's good with you?"

"You know, business as usual. Somebody thought it was okay to park in front of this driveway, so I have to take their vehicle."

"Okay. How long will you be? I'm parked in there." I was anxious to get in my car and call Penelope to tell her about that freak, Kevin.

"Just a few minutes more and I'll be out of your way."

"Okay, thanks. Say, you want to get some coffee or something?" I needed some company, a friendly face to calm me down. Besides, I was dressed and out of the house already, and I wasn't ready to go home and see Roger's face.

"It will take me about a half an hour to take this car to the holding lot. We can meet at the Four Seasons diner on 36 across from the Monmouth Mall."

"I'll be there."

About forty minutes later, the AAA man walked in.

So all I could say was "Hey." I felt stupid because I never got his name.

"How are you?" he asked again.

"I'm good, but you know what, I never got your name."

"And I never got yours either."

"It's Valen."

"Valen, I'm Reid."

"Nice to meet you," we said in unison. We both laughed.

"I guess your job is never done, huh?"

"Nope, it isn't. I could be called out any time of the night for a flat, a tow, someone who locked their keys in the car, or an accident. This is my personal business, so I take a lot of pride in it and don't mind helping people out."

"So you're quite the people person?"

"Yes, you can say that."

The waitress came over and we ordered coffee and Danish.

"Are you married, Reid?"

"No, I'm single."

"Is that by choice?"

"Yes, it is. My job keeps me very busy. Any woman in my life may feel neglected because I'm on call twenty-four hours a day."

"I think that's great that you're aware of that and don't get involved with anyone on a serious level; you're saving some girl a lot of heartache."

Reid was very handsome. He was dressed in his work clothes still, but I could tell that he put some effort into cleaning up to meet me. Our conversation was relaxing. He answered my questions without hesitation, and I appreciated his openness. "Reid, at what point does a man stop loving his wife but refuses to let her go? And why is it that men expect their wives or girlfriends, whichever, to be intimate with them on demand?"

"Since I've never been married, I can't answer that. I can only tell you that if I was involved with a woman and was committed to her, if my feelings ever changed, I would sit her down and tell her. I don't think that it's cool to play with people's emotions."

"Wow! Spoken like a real man. My husband doesn't respect me, desire me, or care how I feel about anything."

"That's too bad. From what I can see, you're a beautiful woman, intelligent, open, and great company."

"Thank you, Mr. Reid." I gave him a little smile.

By the time we were done, it was about eleven. Reid walked me to my car.

"Reid, I had a really nice time. I would like to see you again, if that's okay with you."

"Valen, I'd love to. You still have my card, right?"

"Yes, I do."

"Call me when you can get away."

"I most certainly will."

He leaned in to give me a hug, and we kissed. Even though there was no tongue action, that kiss sent a surge of energy down to my toes.

I kissed him again, almost swallowing his lips this time.

"Wow! Two kisses?"

I kissed him again, this time bringing him closer to me. Whatever had gotten into me was making me step completely out of my box. "Reid?"

"Yes, Valen?"

"Can we go somewhere more private?"

"Where would you like to go?"

"Some place where we can be inside and alone."

"Okay. But can I ask why?"

"Do you have any protection?"

"No, but I can get some."

I pulled back and looked him in the eyes.

He knew what I wanted. "Follow me. I'm parked right over there." Reid pointed to an SUV that was parked at the corner.

"Okay."

We ended up at the Holiday Inn in Eatontown. We sat in the lounge and had a drink.

"Valen, are you sure you want to do this?"

"Yes, Reid, I'm sure." I ordered another round of drinks while he went and paid for the room.

He returned moments later, key dangling in his

hand. "I'm ready if you are, but I need to run to the store in the hotel for condoms."

"Shhhhh!" I laughed. "You're real loud."

"Oh, I'm sorry. Take the key, and I'll meet you up there in a few minutes."

I went ahead upstairs. When I opened the door, I was surprised to see that Reid had gone all out and gotten the room with the Jacuzzi, full bar, and all the amenities a girl could want. I tossed my purse onto the chair that sat by the door and dragged my finger along the marble table that sat beside it. I walked farther into the room. It was absolutely beautiful. Everything was cream. Leather couches, a chaise lounge, and a gorgeous rug brightened up the entire room.

I went over to the tub. It was huge. Numerous jets lined the sides and the bottom of the tub. I turned it on and walked to the bed area. Again, a cream comforter and cream and gold pillows accented the sleigh bed, my favorite. I began to get undressed when there was a knock at the door. I looked through the peephole. When I opened the door, Reid had a brown bag and a handful of wild flowers.

"I know they didn't have this at the store in the hotel."

"No. I had to go a few blocks down to a plaza. Luckily the flower shop was still open." He handed me the brown bag.

"Bubble bath, Magnum condoms. Oh, okay. Nice." I went and poured some bubble bath into the tub.

Reid turned on the radio to the jazz station.

I grabbed one of the robes folded on the bed and went into the bathroom. I returned dressed in the robe, and completely naked under it.

Reid undressed and went into the tub. I joined him, and we sat and had our drinks. "Do you have any fantasies, Reid?"

"Yes. I believe everyone does."

"I have one."

"Just one?"

"One that I really want."

"Okay . . . I'm listening."

"You're going to laugh."

"No, I won't."

"I'd like to perform oral sex."

He choked on his drink. "Wow! Okay. I'm not sure I know what to say."

"Say yes. Let me live out my fantasy with you."

Reid sat his drink down and got up. The bubbles slid down his body. Then he extended his hand.

I looked at his penis. I sat my drink down and allowed him to help me out of the tub.

We dried off, and he went and layed on the bed. I knelt in front of him. I didn't hesitate in fulfilling my fantasy. I took him into my mouth. The feeling of him was liberating. I felt all of the tensions release. All of my insecurities and feelings of inadequacy dissolved, all because Reid allowed me to do me. I licked, sucked, pulled at, and bit on his penis, with my eyes open so that I could see how I was pleasing him.

He held onto my head as I bobbed on his penis. Reid was big, not fat, but long.

I held his penis with one hand and sucked his

balls. I kissed his inner thighs and sucked them as well. After minutes of tasting Reid, I told him, "I want more."

"Okay. Let me slide on a condom."

I climbed onto the bed and watched him as he hooded his penis.

Reid entered me with gentleness. He was caring of my needs as a woman as he kissed my skin, touched my hair and said things to me that every woman should hear. "You are so beautiful."

"Reid, you feel so good."

We made love for hours. It was about three in the morning when I decided to go home. "Reid," I whispered as he slept, "I have to go." I got out of the bed.

"Why?"

That's a good question. I ended up climbing back into bed with him until checkout time the next morning.

Chapter 26

Lyda

Terry called me and invited me to dinner again. This time I told him that I would take him to dinner. Since he'd given me that money, I'd paid off all my bills and pre-paid them for three months.

Meanwhile, Anthony had been calling me like crazy, and Boyfriend was his usual self.

"Jalisa, you should come out with me to dinner with Terry. He's a really nice guy, and fun too."

"Why would I want to be a third wheel on your date with Terry?"

"Girl, I'm paying, so third wheel or not, you should come."

"Okay. I'll go."

We'd decided to go to Delta's again. Terry, Jalisa, and I got there around eight or so. We had to wait for a table, so we took a seat at the bar and had drinks.

"So how long have you guys been friends?" Terry asked.

"A long time," said Jalisa. "We've been through a lot together."

"That's nice."

"Yes, Terry. Jalisa, she's a great girl, sweet, dedicated, horny."

"Excuse me, Lyda?"

"Damn!" Terry laughed.

"I can't believe you, Lyda, but then again, nothing you say should surprise me."

"So is she right?"

"Yes, I'm a sweet girl."

"No, heifer, he wants to know if you're horny."

"Well, isn't everyone, at some point or another?"

"There, you have it." I said.

"So what do you when you're horny, Jalisa?" Terry asked.

"Normal people have sex, you know, but I have a husband who could care less about pleasing me so I'm on my own. It's nothing a few batteries can't cure."

"Well, give me a dollar and try your luck. Ask your girl what happened when she gave me a dollar."

"I know. That is so wild. I can't believe you hit that big."

"Life is good I must admit."

"Okay enough of the corny flirting are you two feeling any chemistry between each other?"

Terry laughed it off. "Lyda, you are tripping."

I looked at Jalisa. I could tell she was trying to

see if there was anything in him that she found remotely interesting. I nudged her under the table.

She looked at me and gave me a wink.

"I have to use the ladies room." I excused myself
from the table.

"Is she always this blunt?" Terry asked Jalisa.

"Brother, you have no idea. So what do you do
Terry?"

"Right now, nothing. And I'll probably be doing
that for a little bit more."

"I know that's right. If I won money like that, I
would definitely take a moment to breathe, go
away for a few weeks, and just relax. Maybe take a
walk on the wild side and go away on one of those
nudist vacations."

"Wow! Really? So is this something you've been
thinking about lately, or has this been a long-time
fantasy of yours?"

"Terry, I'm married, as I'm sure you already
know. We're just not working out, he's not into
pleasing me, and I'm not into dealing with it. I've
made up my mind that I'll have to take care of me,
so whether it is a recent fantasy or not, it is something that I would do if I had the chance."

"Jalisa, I know we just met, but I'd like to see you
again."

"I'd like that, Terry. Here's my business card."

"So you're a tailor?"

"Yes. I make clothes too. I also have a girl out in
California who helps me. Speaking of which, I
need to take a trip out there."

"What are you doing tomorrow night?"

"Nothing. Quinton will be at the restaurant, and I'll be home as usual."

"Okay. I'll call you tomorrow morning, and we'll decide on a time and place."

"Sounds good to me."

I came back and could tell that they'd at least talked about getting together. Terry was a really nice guy, and Jalisa was my girl. If I could get her some dick, then my job was done. I mean I thought about getting with Terry, but I just didn't get that spark from him.

"Lyda, Jalisa agreed to see me in the near future."

"All right. That's cool. When?"

"We're thinking about tomorrow evening. Maybe I'll have him over for dinner."

"Dinner where? Your place?"

Jalisa nodded her head yes.

"And what about Quinton?"

"Quinton is your husband, I presume."

"Yes, he is, but he won't be there. He's never there. I'm not worried, so it's settled. My place, let's say, around seven?"

"I'll be there."

"Can I come?" I wanted to be there when Jalisa pulled that off.

"Sure. I'll pick up a few bottles of wine and order from the bistro on Broadway. I will not be cooking; we're really going to chill."

Damn! I was impressed with the new Jalisa. She invited Terry into her home, the same home that

Quinton claimed he provided for her, the same home that she'd laid up in alone all too many nights, longing for her man. Umph, it was gonna be some funky mess up in there.

Chapter 27

Jalisa

I asked Quinton, "I take it tonight will be another late night for you?"

"No, I don't think so. I should be home around eleven. I told you that my manager in training was doing well and didn't need me there."

"Okay. I was just checking. So eleven, right?" I wanted to give him the impression that I would be waiting. If tonight was like any other night, he'd find some reason to stay at the restaurant. I pressed more to ensure it. "Quinton, please don't be late. If you tell me eleven, then eleven is when I'll be expecting you."

"Jalisa, I said, 'eleven' damn!"

"I just want to make sure."

I knew my plan was working when he stormed out of the kitchen. I could guarantee he wasn't going to come home when he said he would.

Lyda had gotten there early. I had asked her to

pick up the food because I was still straightening up. Neither one of us had heard from Valen, which was strange.

"Maybe she's on a date. I'm still trippin' on that mess."

"Yeah well, Lyda, we're fed up. You have it easy because you're not married to anyone. So whenever you're tired, all you have to do is send them home."

"I know. But that's not all it's cracked up to be. Not having someone with me every night gets lonely. I wish I could find someone who could fulfill me completely. Maybe I was just meant to be single."

"You could have someone home with you every night, Lyda, but they may not necessarily meet your needs. I'm just saying that you have options without consequences."

"Well, you're being pretty bold by exercising your options to have company, male company, no less. What would you do if Quinton came home and saw Terry here?"

"Nothing. He would be *your* friend. I wouldn't do a damn thing but laugh my ass off."

Terry showed up at seven on the dot with desserts, tiramisu and a fruit salad.

"Come on in, Terry, and welcome."

"Hey, ladies? What's happening?"

Lyda opened a bottle of Mondavi Chardonnay and poured us all a glass. We went and sat in the living room. Lyda sat in the chair, while Terry and I took the couch.

"Really nice place, Jalisa."

"Thanks. I like it."

"Yeah, Jalisa, you're satisfied, right?"

"Ha ha, Lyda."

"What?" Terry asked.

"It's just that my husband feels that, since he provides me with this home and pays most of the bills, I shouldn't have one complaint. Not one."

"Do you have any complaints?"

"Yes," Lyda began, "he don't f—"

"Lyda, I got this."

Lyda laughed. "Look at this," she said as she went to refill her glass, "I'm out of wine."

"So do you have any complaints?" Terry asked again.

"Yes. Before we got married, Quinton and I were great. We meshed, and I felt like he was my soul mate. A few months after we got married, things changed, he stopped being attentive, stopped showing any type of affection. The ironic thing is that he got me by being compassionate, letting me know that he desired me and loved me. Now, I don't feel any connection to him on any level, and when I bring it up, he thinks I nag. So I stopped bringing it up and accepted the fact that I'm in control of my own happiness."

"Too many men make that mistake. I see it in my homeboys, both married and single, and I just shake my head in disbelief."

"Do you have a girlfriend?"

"No. I'm not ready for commitment, I just want to have fun."

Lyda said as she came and sat down. "My sentiments exactly."

I sat back as Lyda and Terry engaged in a conversation about sex and the free will to have it. I
thought about my situation. Lyda's and Valen's
too.

A year ago, neither Valen nor I would've considered having extra-marital affairs. Now she was an
escort, and I was on my way to being a justified ho.
I laughed out loud. The wine relaxed me, and I
just listened to Terry and Lyda talk.

"Lyda, why don't you go and try to call Valen?"

"Okay, girl. Of course."

Lyda knew the deal. When she was out of the
room, I turned to Terry. "Terry, you want to play?"

"Word!"

I went into the kitchen, where Lyda was on the
phone with Valen. "You did what with who?"

"Girl, she done did it to the AAA man," Lyda
whispered to me.

"What!" I busted out laughing. "When? Where?"

"The Holiday Inn? This morning? Get it, girl."
Lyda did her hump dance. I knew then that Valen
had done some crazy mess.

I tapped Lyda on her shoulder. "Tell her you'll
call her from the car."

She looked at me. "What?" she mouthed silently.

I did her hump dance to let her know I was
about to get it on with Terry.

"Oh lawd! Between the two of you, y'all got me
beat. Valen, I'll call you from the car." She hung
up the phone. "You two are about to do it? Damn,
I leave the room and now you're about to get some
dick. Go ahead, girl; I'm not mad at you."

Terry walked Lyda out to the car, at which point
I put the food that we didn't get a chance to eat

away and washed out the glasses. I dried the dishes and put them away. *Quinton wouldn't know anything.* I made sure to leave no evidence behind.

As Terry came back into the house, I stood on the stairs. "Lock the door behind you and meet me upstairs," I told him.

When he got up there, I was already undressed and on the bed.

"Oh damn!"

"Just come here, Terry. If you think you hit the jackpot with your lottery winnings, wait until you play this hot slot."

Chapter 28

Valen

"Girl, he was pissed. He looked at me like I was crazy when I walked in the door this morning. I didn't say one word. I just looked at him back and went upstairs to get a shower."

"He didn't say anything?"

"Nope. He just looked at me."

"Wow! I don't believe this shit. You and Jalisa are off the chain."

"Why? What did she do?" I laughed because I could imagine what it was if Lyda had a hand in it.

"Right now, Terry is fucking the shit out of her."

"Who?"

"Terry, the dude that won the lottery and gave me that money."

"Oh my gosh! Are you serious?"

"As hell. You two keep it up and you'll have just as many notches on your belt, if not more than I do."

"Oh, that will never happen, not with me anyway."

"How can you say that? You're all working for an escort service and what not."

"Speaking of which, I had a nutcase last night. I called the agency and told them that they need to do a better job screening these people before they hook me up again."

"You can never be too sure about anybody these days, Valen. Just be careful and protect yourself. I'm going home. I'll get with you later."

After I hung up with Lyda, I went to make a cup of tea. Roger was sitting in his office, and as I walked by, I saw him sitting at his desk with his head in his hands. I kept walking. He'd made his bed and now he had to lie in it. I wasn't going to put this fire out like I used to do in the past. I was always the one who wanted to work through things, not go to bed angry, and make peace when things were bad. Not any more. I was so done. And I think he knew this.

After I made my tea, I was on my way back to my room when he called out to me. "Come in here please."

I ignored him and continued to go to my room. My plans for the evening were to meet up with Haze and have dinner and maybe catch a movie. I wasn't interested in Roger stressing me out.

He screamed. "Valen!"

Why did he think I would respond? He just didn't get it. He messed our whole arrangement up. All the time he thought he was being the man of the house, demanding this and that, thinking that I owed him something, while our marriage was dying right under his nose. I heard him coming, so I braced myself for a confrontation.

"How can I put this . . . as long as you're my wife, you will not come in this house a day after you leave it. Valen, you're playing a game that could potentially be very dangerous."

"Roger, don't threaten me." I reached for the phone.

"It's not a threat, Valen. You're not going to disrespect me in my own house."

I dialed Haze's phone number. " 'Disrespect'? You don't want to talk about disrespect."

Haze answered the phone.

"Hey, what time would be good for you?"

Roger stood there in disbelief that I would begin another conversation while he was trying to make a point that would go missed on my part.

"Okay, I'll meet you there." I hung up the phone.

"You're still upset about the doll? Valen, I could've been doing worse."

"No, Roger, I'm not upset." I walked over to my closet to find something to wear."

"Who was that on the phone?"

"Who do you think it was?" I knew he would never think that I had the nerve to call and speak with another man right in his face. *And our men think they know us.*

"See, you spend too much time with those cackling-hen friends of yours, that's why you're all messed up; you listen to them like they know what's best for you and my household."

"Yes, you've made it quite clear that this is your household." I pulled out a pair of jeans, black silk turtleneck, and then I reached for my boots.

"You damn right this is my house. And like I said, you won't be coming in here like you did this morning."

I walked away from him. Nothing he said to me meant anything. He could huff and puff and do whatever he wanted, I was going to go out with Haze, and I was going to get home when I got there.

We met at Flava's again. This time we got a table and ordered dinner. Our conversation was great and I felt great. During the evening, Haze took my hands and gently rubbed them. He touched my face and complimented me on how I looked. "You look different from when we last saw each other."

"I know. I *am* different."

We ate our food then took a ride over to Jersey Gardens. We wanted to see a movie, but all of the early shows were sold out. And since neither one of us wanted to catch the late show, Haze suggested that we go to his place.

"Okay. I think we can do that. I'll follow you."

When I got in the car, I called Lyda and Jalisa to tell them where I was going. Earlier I had stopped at Walgreen's to pick up a few things to keep in my car for an event like this. I called it my "cheat kit." It consisted of condoms, vaginal wipes, body wipes, booty spray, a toothbrush and toothpaste, a pair of panties, mints, a comb, brush, an extra key to the house and my car, and an extra cell phone. So I was set as I followed Haze to his house.

I could definitely tell that there was no consistent woman in his life. Haze's spot had "man" written all over it. Music memorabilia covered the walls. He had a studio in one of the rooms, and there was music equipment and tons of CD's everywhere.

"Make yourself at home. It's small, but it's comfortable."

Haze was right. I took off my boots and sat on the couch.

He went into the kitchen and came out with two beers.

"Thanks." I took the beer from him.

"What's that?" He pointed to my cheat kit.

"It's just girl stuff."

"Oh okay." He sat back and took a sip of his beer.

I stared at him and he at me. He looked so cute in his basketball jersey, jeans, and Timberland boots. I'd never dated or been with anyone like Haze. He was thugged out and I loved it; it was exciting to me.

I took the bottle of beer to my mouth, tilted the bottle back, and took a long drink. I let out a burp.

He shifted in his seat. "Wow! That's all you got?" He took a drink of his, nearly all of it, and let out one that made me burst out laughing.

"Damn! I'll give you a ten for that."

He laughed and got up to get two more.

I took it and sat it on the floor next to me. I proceeded to take the opened bottle and put it in my mouth. Haze watched me as I slid it in and out, making sure I got it wet. I made sounds with my saliva and looked directly at him as I sucked the neck of it.

"That's all you got?"

"Nope."

"So what's good then?"

"Us."

"That's what's up."

We finished our beers and retreated to his bedroom. To my surprise, it was clean. The bed was made with white sheets and a throw blanket. He had more music stuff on the walls in there and tons of jewelry on his dresser.

"These are nice. Bet they cost a lot of money."

"Some. Others were gifts as payments. I don't wear a lot of jewelry often, just on special occasions."

"I see." I sat on his bed.

He came and leaned into me. We fell back and began to kiss. Haze was so gentle. His lips were soft and wet.

I spread my legs so that he could lay between them. I felt his hard dick pressed against me. I wanted it right then. "Get up."

He did as I asked.

I took his pants down then his boxers. My mouth watered for the taste of his hard dick.

"Go 'head," he said in a sexy voice. His breathing was heavy and I could tell he wanted it just as much as I did.

I licked it from the bottom up. I felt it pulsating, getting larger by each lick. When I took him into my mouth entirely, I felt him pump his dick into my mouth. I watched him as he let me devour him with each suck.

He closed his eyes and moaned in approval of my tongue.

"You like it?"

"Hell yeah, Valen. Damn! I could feel you like this every day."

"Yeah? Tell me how to suck it."

"Baby, take it all in your mouth."

I did, and he let out a groan of pleasure. I sucked him so good that he came not once, but twice back to back. I wasn't undressed yet but quickly changed that. I pulled out a condom from my cheat kit and tossed it to him.

"Now we can get down to business."

Four condoms later, Haze had sexed me up in ways that I'd only imagined. *Lyda would be proud of me.*

We lay in the bed together and held each other.

"What are you looking for, Valen?"

"I used to look to fall in love, Haze. Right now, I'm not looking for anything but to be loved. I'm tired of making sure everyone is taken care of at my expense." I looked up at him. "You understand what I'm saying?"

"Yes, I do. How about another beer, baby?"

"Thanks. That would be great."

Chapter 29

Lyda

When I got home, Boyfriend was waiting for me outside. I didn't like when my men did that, just pop up without calling before. I wished they would call me and tell me that they were going to meet me at my spot. Their feelings would've been hurt if I pulled up with another dude in the car. Then *I* would be real wrong.

"What's up? What are you doing here?"

"I thought we could just relax for a while."

"Well," I lied, "I told Charletta that we could chill out tonight." I hated being put on the spot, and his showing up did that.

"You can do that. I'll chill here, and you can go over to her place."

I could tell that I wasn't going to get rid of him that easy. I opened the front door, and we went inside. If I didn't know he was going to fuck me like crazy later on, I would've sent him on his way.

I went and changed into something more comfortable. I hated just popping up at Charletta's house unannounced, but Boyfriend kind of got on my nerves with his unexpected visit.

"Okay, I'll be next door for a few. Make yourself at home," I said, as if I needed to tell him that. Boyfriend already had his shoes off and lay across my couch with the remote in one hand and the phone in the other.

When I got to Charletta's, she'd just finished cooking dinner. The kids had already had their bath and were watching television in their room. She had candles going and the radio on as she cleaned up the dinner dishes.

"Hey Charletta, I know we didn't plan to get together, but I just needed to unwind a little."

"Girl, you don't have to have an excuse to come and chill out. I told you before, anything you need, all you have to do is ask."

"Thanks, girl. What I need right now is to just relax. Got any wine?"

"Yes. I always have that." She opened the kitchen cabinet above the stove.

"Red or white?"

"White. Preferably Chardonnay."

She opened the bottle, and we had a glass of wine.

Charletta seemed to be holding up pretty well with her situation.

"How are you doing, Charletta?"

"Girl, some days are better than others."

"I would've cut him personally," I said.

"Yeah, I hear you, but what would that solve? He cheated, and now he's paying big. I'm in his pockets for years to come. I was heart-broken, but everything happens for a reason. I've always believed that. Besides, I have these two kids that need their mother. What would they do without me? What good would I be to them if I'm in jail behind some trifling fool who couldn't keep his dick in his pants?"

"I do too. I do believe that everyone creates their own karma."

She hadn't dated since her divorce. I guess the kids took a lot of her time. She was a great mother. We weren't that close, but every time I saw her, she was in good spirits, always smiling when she was with her kids.

Charletta excused herself so that she could check on the kids. When she returned, she poured another glass of wine and invited me to chill with her in her bedroom. "Don't think I'm crazy, but I just bought this new television. It's a flat screen that I had mounted on the wall. It has a great picture."

Okay, I did a little, but she'd never given me any reason to think anything foul about her. "Oh no, I didn't think that."

When she turned on the television, *Unfaithful* with Richard Gere was on. I didn't know if that movie was appropriate, so I asked, "Do you have BET?"

"I do, but this is one of my all-time favorite movies. It's a shame how that man killed that young boy. He wasn't doing anything that the wife didn't want him to do. She was the one creeping. That man loved his wife. I wished I got that from my loser of a husband."

"Charletta, some men aren't capable of loving like that. My friends complain all the time about how their men feel like material things can compensate for being loved. I wonder if they learn that from their childhood. You know, some boys who don't get enough love from their mother grow up to be men who can't show their women any emotional commitment. They do that by smothering them with the material things and expect them to be happy."

"I know. I need that emotional connection."

We sat back and watched the movie. I thought about Charletta's last comment about needing the emotional connection. I didn't see where that would do me any good. I'd seen men do some trifling things. Hell, I'd had them done to me, but because I didn't have any emotional bond, they really didn't phase me. I gave them their walking papers and sent them on their way. I wondered if I'd be that way forever, or would my knight in shining armor come and rescue me from my inability to commit?

Commitment is a lot of work. And if you really thought about it, I'd somewhat committed to Boyfriend because he was a constant in my life, no matter what. Between flings, there was Boyfriend, and sometimes he was there during.

"Wow! First she fell in the middle of a windstorm; now he has her in his sheets."

"They do look sexy together, you have to admit." I turned and faced Charletta and leaned up on my elbows. "Do you ever think you will have another committed relationship again?"

"I hope so; I love being in a relationship. I'm lonely the way things are, but I need to keep it on point because of the kids. The last thing they need is a mother who can't stop having sex to validate her womanhood, when their father has cheated them of so much already."

"I would imagine it's lonely. I'm so used to having someone in my life that if I had no one, I wouldn't know what to do."

"Well, hopefully one day I'll find that special someone who can fill the void in my life on an emotional level."

I looked at Charletta closely for the first time. Her long, relaxed hair framed her narrow face. She had soft features and smooth skin. She was attractive. "Don't you ever want to have sex?" I laughed. I didn't know why I was embarrassed.

"Yes, I do. But that's what these are for." Charletta went into her closet and pulled out a bag with dildos, different-size batteries, flavored warming gel, and a few porno DVD's.

"Oh shit! I would never have guessed."

"Why? Because I look all innocent and sweet? I'm sweet but definitely not innocent."

"Hummmm." That was very interesting to me. I had a freak for a neighbor. Charletta wasn't beat for getting her groove on. Since I didn't have a bag of tricks, I wanted to try what she had. "What's that like?" I pointed to the raspberry gel.

"This is one of my favorites." She pulled it out, squirted out about the size of a pea, and rubbed it on my hand.

It was warm.

"Now taste it."

I tasted it and it wasn't bad. In fact it had a

numbing effect. I couldn't feel my tongue like I normally could.

Charletta laughed as I softly chomped on it. "This one is good in case you want to give head and not gag. And this is the dick I suck when I just want to be straight-up nasty." Charletta pulled out a dick that was absolutely every woman's dream. It had veins, a head with a little hole in it, and a pair of nuts.

"Charletta, doll, you are blowing my mind."

"Want to try it?"

"Try it? Uh, I don't know about that. Don't *you* use it?"

"Yes, but I clean it after I do. You'll be okay. Let me use it on you."

Okay, now she's really buggin'. In all of my play experience, I'd never been with a woman before.

"You aren't scared, are you?" she asked in a soft and sultry voice.

"No."

"Let me check on the kids one more time then we'll play, okay?"

"Okay." I thought I was strictly "dickly," but Charletta had me curious. I went for the bottle of wine and brought it back into the bedroom with me.

Charletta returned shortly thereafter. "They're asleep. Let's take a shower."

Charletta turned on the music while I started the shower. We got undressed and got in. Charletta took the soap, lathered it, and began to wash me. I got turned on. The motions she made with her hands were relaxing. She rubbed my breasts, turned me around and washed my back, then she told me to bend over.

"For what?"

"Just turn around. I want to wash you here." She reached around and gently poked my asshole.

"Okay," I said willingly.

Charletta took the suds that she'd made and wiped me from the front to the back several times, gently flicking my clit as she did that. She knew exactly what she was doing and knew that I was getting more aroused with every touch of her hands.

After she washed me, I returned the favor.

Charletta turned the water down to a steady drip and told me to hold on to the sides of the shower. She knelt down in front of me and parted my legs. "You ready?" She had a devilish grin on her face.

By then I was panting from excitement and nervousness. "Yes." No one ever had me under control like Charletta did. She was making everything happen. She had me open.

I wasn't shaven, so it took a few licks before I felt the warmth of her tongue. It felt like it was wide and that she was taking the entire outside of my pussy into her mouth.

She licked and flicked while I tried to hold on to the wet walls.

I leaned back and lifted my leg higher so that she could enjoy all of me. It felt so good and sensual. The way she slipped and slid on me made me wonder about what I'd been missing all these years.

"How does that feel?" She looked at me and stuck her tongue out. It must've been special order because it was like four inches long and was as wide as I'd imagined it to be.

I let my head fall back. "Good. Don't stop." I wanted more. I wanted this water off me and Charletta all over me.

I turned off the shower and helped her to her feet. I kissed her on the lips and tasted my juices. I licked my lips and reached down between her legs. Either all the water went directly there, or she was just that wet. "Wow! Eating me out did that to you?"

She nodded yes. "Let's go back to the bedroom." She stepped out of the shower and handed me a towel, and we dried each other off.

Charletta closed the door behind her.

I sat on the bed, and she sat next to me. I leaned down and took her nipple in my mouth.

Charletta gripped my head. "You're teasing me the right way."

Since I'd never done that before, I needed her to tell me that I was pleasing her like she pleased me by licking the shit out of my pussy. She fell back, and I got on top of her. Her legs spread as if they were on remote control, and I fell between. I could feel the heat coming from her; it was a complete turn-on.

We kissed passionately. Our tongues were strangers, but you wouldn't have known that by the way they played. She took my tongue and sucked it; I opened my mouth wide enough for her to take the whole thing. I tried to take hers and do the same, but it was too big. She had it going on with the tongue.

"Let me taste you." I moved over to one of her

breasts. They weren't perfect breasts; after all she was a mother of two, but she definitely had some sex appeal going on with her. I slowly slid down her body, planting little kisses along the way. She made sounds of pleasure as I stopped at her belly button. I stuck my tongue inside of it and gently sucked as I moved farther down.

By then, she had her knees bent and her feet on the bed.

I pulled back to see what she looked like, golden, with a hint of brownness was the color of her lips. She was clean-shaven, with the exception of a little pointed patch at the top of her lips. I spread them and began to taste her moistness. "You taste so good." I let my face fall all the way into her and went to work on one of the tastiest fruits I'd ever eaten.

I licked Charletta's pussy in different places and got completely different responses from her. She was enjoying what I was doing to her.

"Lyda, let me get it."

I knew what she was talking about. She wanted to get that "king kong" of a dildo and fuck me with it. "Okay. Do you have any KY jelly?"

"Yes." Charletta got up off of the bed and reached into her nightstand. "And we can't forget this." She pulled out this strappy thing.

"What is that for?"

"It's going to hold this." She held up the dildo, "so that I can please you from a woman's point of view."

Man, I was like, *how the hell could a freak like me miss noticing the freak in Charletta?* No, we didn't hang like that, but normally freaks recognized freaks, whether it was from something they said or did, we picked up on that shit. None of that mattered, though. I was about to get me some new and different type of dick, so I was all good. I watched Charletta twist, turn, and mount the strap on her hips.

A couple moves later, she was walking around like a well-hung he-she. "You want it?"

"Damn straight."

Charletta mounted me and started stoking like she'd been doing this all her life.

I held on tight as she gripped my hips so that they wouldn't slide all over the bed. I took her like she was my man, and for the moment she was. I had to give it to her, she was tearing this ass up. "Umph . . . Charletta . . . Damn it, girl, take this pussy!"

"You never had this before, have you? I see you and all of your men coming in and out and I knew that they weren't satisfying you. I could tell because if they were, you would've had only one."

"Um hum," was all I could say.

"So I waited. I knew that something would give me the opportunity, and you did that tonight. Do you mind what I'm doing to you?"

"No. Keep doing me. Keep fucking me."

"Whose is this?"

"What?"

"Whose pussy is this?"

"Oh no, you didn't."

She was trying to claim my ass. "Tell me. Say it."

"Fuck it, it's yours. This is your pussy."

Chapter 30

Jalisa

Terry and I didn't waste any time. The minute we got into the bedroom, we were all over each other. He ripped off my clothes, and I did the same. We fell onto the bed, and he immediately put it in. I was lost in the excitement of both getting some sex and getting it in my husband's bedroom. I managed to scoot up far enough to pull the covers back.

Terry wasn't gentle. In fact, he was a little more rambunctious than I would've liked him to be, even though the sex was good.

"Terry, you didn't put on a condom."

"I'm good, baby."

"No. Wait." I tried to sit up.

"For what? I'm already in there, baby girl. You know you like it. You don't want me to stop doing this, do you?" He began to stroke me slowly then he kissed me.

I gave in to his pressure. "No."

"All right. Then let me take care of this ass. You shouldn't have to go without some good dick."

Terry was right. I'd gone long enough without being made to feel like I was a woman. A woman who deserved to be loved. A woman who'd been neglected but was making up for lost time. I didn't feel like I got my just due yet, so I fucked Terry for hours until we both were too exhausted to move.

"You were great," he said as we lay in the bed. He was on Quinton's side; I was on mine.

"You weren't so bad yourself. Do you realize that you're laying in my husband's bed?"

"Yeah, and . . . ? If he was handling you right, I wouldn't be here."

"This is so true. I'm going to take a shower." I went into the bathroom. I looked myself in the mirror and stared at the person I'd become.

Six months ago, I was this dedicated wife, making every effort to make sure that my husband was good. I took his blows of rejection, thinking that he'd get it one day. That day never came. "Oh well," I said out loud.

I took a quick shower, douched, and dried off. I wrapped myself in a towel and went back into the bedroom. Terry was already dressed. "You don't want to take a quick shower?"

"Nah, I'm good. I'm about to go home; I'll get right there."

"Are you sure?" I asked, kind of grossed out.

"Yeah. Now come here and give me a kiss."

I did, and we gave each other a hug. I walked him downstairs and saw him out. Then I closed the door behind me and took a moment to reflect on what had just happened.

"I think I'll go down to the restaurant to get something to eat."

When I got there, it was empty. There were a few people having dinner, but compared to how it'd been the last two times I'd been there, there wasn't anything happening. Darrell wasn't the host. There was a young lady there that night.

"May I have a table for one, please?"

"It'll be fifteen minutes." She spoke without looking up at me.

" 'Fifteen minutes'? The place is empty. Why do I have to wait fifteen minutes?"

She walked away without answering.

I swear the young kids these days have no respect for adults. I can't believe that Quinton allows these types of people to work in his place. I made a mental note to ask him about that.

The rude little girl returned, grabbed a menu, and asked me to follow her. She tossed the menu on the table and walked away.

I'd had enough of that little heifer and her attitude. "Excuse me is there any reason why you're so nasty?"

"No, excuse *me*, you asked for a table for one, and you got it. Your waiter will be with you shortly." She turned as she said *shortly*.

"I want to see the manager."

She stopped in her tracks and turned back around. "The manager? Oh really?" She walked back to me. "Do you mean Quinton?"

"Yes, I do, my husband, Quinton. Get him, please, because I've just about had it with you and your funky attitude."

She reached for a walkie-talkie that was connected to her belt. "Ah, Quinton, we have a disgruntled customer here."

"Thank you!" I had major attitude going on. *That little bitch should've stayed home if she didn't want to come to work today.* It wasn't my problem that all she knew to do was seat people.

When she walked away, she took her time and added a funky switch to her stride.

Quinton came from out of the kitchen and walked into her. He touched her arms then her cheek.

Then she turned around and pointed to me.

I got up. "That's right, Quinton. Get over here now."

He came like a dog with his tail between his legs.

I swore, sometimes I could've kicked myself for marrying such an asshole. I wanted to smack him so bad, but the scene I was about to make was going to be more than good enough. "Why are you touching all over her like that?"

"What? What are you talking about? Why do you always have to have some type of drama going on? We have it at home, and now you bringing it to my business, my workplace?"

"Oh, I'm bringing it, all right. Is that what's been keeping you here to the wee hours of the morning? You fucking her?" I wasn't loud—yet.

"Lower your voice, Jalisa; you're making a fool of yourself."

"I'm making a fool of myself? Ha! Quinton, you've got to be kidding me. All this time I wondered why you weren't intimate with me and it all comes down to the fact that you're fucking a teenager."

"First of all, Jalisa, she's not a teenager. She's a

senior in high school and works here as the night-time manager. That's the one that I was training all that time. Secondly, I'm not having sex with her. So I'd appreciate it if you either sit down and order some food or order your food and leave; you're disturbing the other patrons."

I sat down. "Send my waiter over here, Quinton, before I tear this place up."

Just as I said that, the little funky ass came trotting over with a smirk on her face. In a few more minutes, I was going to slap it right off.

"What are you looking at?"

"You must be the missus. It's nice to meet you finally." She extended her hand, fake nails and all.

"Don't play yourself, little girl. I'm not to be messed with. Quinton, you better get your manager before she gets managed."

"You're not going to manage nobody. Quinton is my man. What's he gonna do with you when he can have this?" She moved her hands over her body like she was straight from the streets.

Quinton grabbed her by the arm and pulled her away.

She was still talking mess. "No, fuck that. She come in here thinking she's all that. I'm not the one, you better tell that bitch, or I will."

Quinton managed to pull her into the back.

Just as they disappeared, Darrell appeared.

I was heated. I knew full well that if I hit that little girl, I would hurt her and probably go to jail. Who did this wench think she was?

Darrell looked as Quinton took her to the back and then looked over in my direction. I was too pissed to wave to him, but he saw me and came over.

"What's up, sexy? What was that all about?"

"That young girl must not be feeling well today. She's was a little rude, to say the least."

"She's a trip, trust me."

"What does that mean?"

"Oh, um . . . did I open my big mouth?"

"Ah yes, you did, and it better stay open and flowing with the answer to my question."

"Wow! I always do that."

I'd heard enough. Darrell didn't have to say another word for me to read between the lines. He wanted to tell me that Quinton was fucking this chick but couldn't, so I helped him out. "How long, Darrell?"

"Since she started here and even more so when she began training as a manager."

"And how long is that? Don't talk in riddles; you weren't talking in riddles when you were all up in my ass."

"She's been training about eight weeks."

" 'Eight weeks'? Eight fuckin' weeks?" I grabbed my purse and got up. I made a beeline to the front and then went right to the kitchen. There was Quinton and Miss Hoochie Momma all hugged up kissing and what not. "You are so fucked up. Why, Quinton? All this time I tried to figure out what was wrong with our marriage. This is it? Is this the best you could do? A little girl?" I shouted as I walked up on him and his ho.

I smacked the mess out of him and commenced to wiping the stainless steel counter top with that chick. I had her hair and yanked her neck because, Lord knows, I was trying to break it. She fell to the floor, and I spat right in her face. Then I turned and spat in Quinton's.

Darrell had come in at that very moment. The look on his face was great. He didn't seem to know whether to call 911 or laugh.

I heard little missy trying to get up, so I turned around and warned her. "Your best bet is to stay where you are before I whip on your ass some more."

"Jalisa, you've gone too far."

"Really? Oh well . . . Darrell, what you got planned for the night? Let's get out of here."

"Umph, Mr. Quinton, boy, I don't know. Ms. Jalisa is fine as wine, and I love being all up in that behind. See ya! Oh and I quit, can't work for Mr. Bossman and be screwing his wife now, could I?"

Chapter 31

Valen

Haze and I put away ten beers between the two of us. I wasn't a beer drinker, so needless to say, I was hit. We lay in his bed and looked at each other. Haze was a fine chocolate brother. He had smooth skin, a sexy stomach, and muscular legs. He was younger than I was though, and I imagined if we ever got serious, we'd have some issues.

"Fatal Haze, now I see why."

He looked over at me with the sexiest eyes and rubbed the back of my head. "What's good, baby?"

I loved it when he called me baby. "If I wasn't careful, I could get used to that kind of lovin'." I felt like I could tell him that.

"Haze, how do you really feel about me and how you met me? I can't see where you would ever forget the circumstances in which we met. I'm sure you'll agree that we have a great time together, but you do know this is all it could ever be, right?"

"You may be right, Valen, but then again you may be wrong. People come into other people's lives for different reasons. We won't know that reason until we're meant to know."

"I guess so."

I thought about calling Lyda and Jalisa so that they wouldn't worry, but if they were worried, they would've called me by now. Since they didn't, I assumed that all was well on their end.

I curled up next to Haze and fell asleep.

Morning came quickly. I had a serious headache, and my mouth was dry. I reached over to try and feel for Haze, but he wasn't there. Then I smelled the delicious aroma of food. I got up and put on one of his white T-shirts. Then I went out of the room and into the kitchen.

His place wasn't that big, so when you walked out of the bedroom, you were in the living room/dining area. I saw him standing in front of the stove in his boxers.

"Umm . . . something smells good." I said as I went up behind him.

He took his fingers and stuck them in my vagina then put them up to his nose. "Damn sure do, baby. I was just about to put these biscuits in the oven."

"Okay. I'll be on the couch." I grabbed the remote that sat on the small coffee table and turned on the television.

Haze came right behind me and sat next to me on the couch. "Sleep well?"

"I haven't slept like that in a long time, but I assume it's because I was a little drunk. Do you have any aspirin?" The room began to spin a little.

"Yes, baby. Lay down while I get it."

Haze was a gentleman. When he spoke to me, he spoke with respect, and when I spoke he listened. He came back with a glass of orange juice and the aspirins.

"Thank you, Haze." Drifting in and out of sleep, I leaned on Haze's chest and could feel his breath on my face.

"Just lay back and relax. We're not in any rush." He had his hand on my hair and rubbed the crown of my head every so often. He slid from behind me and laid me down all the way. "Valen."

"Hm?"

"Baby, I want to feel you."

I smiled a sleepy smile. My eyes were closed as I pulled him up and on top of me and spread my legs.

I could feel him pull himself out of his boxers. When entered me, it was as if we hadn't had sex at all. I was so tight and he was so hard. I grabbed onto him and held him as tight as I could.

"Valen, this dick could be yours if you want it."

I didn't know what to say. All I knew was that he made me feel so damn good. The way he loved me was intoxicating. Just as drug addicts stayed out for days when they were on their "get-high" kicks, I saw myself staying in his apartment for days too.

He touched my chin. "Valen, talk to me, baby. Baby?" He stopped stroking me.

"Yes, Fatal Haze."

"What would make you happy? What can I do to let you know that I want to be in your life?"

"Haze, you can't do anything. I've enjoyed our time together immensely. I'm a married woman. Before anything can really happen, I need to be divorced. And Roger will put up a fight if I served him with any kind of divorce papers."

"So what? I don't care; I want you here with me."

He said all the right things. Haze touched me all the right ways, but the fact was, I didn't want anybody on a serious level after Roger. I needed time to find myself, to do me. Travel. Maybe date some more to see what was out there.

"You hear me?" He put his hand under my shirt and rubbed my stomach. Then he moved up to my breasts and began to stroke me again.

I relaxed and allowed him to take me as he wanted.

He slid off of the couch and kneeled in front of me.

"Taste me," I begged him.

His tongue lit my clit on fire. Its rapid movements sent chills up my legs and all through my pelvic area.

I grinded to meet his desire and came within minutes. "Can you taste it?"

"Yes, baby. I taste you." Haze got up. "Turn around."

I positioned myself so that the top half of my body was leaning over the back of the couch and my ass was in the air. I felt him lick me from behind then he entered me with fierceness.

"Oh shit, Valen, I could love you like this every night."

"You make me feel so good, Haze."

We made love for another hour or so. By the time we were done, I couldn't move.

"Haze, the biscuits!"

"Oh, you're right." He jumped up and ran to the oven. "Just in time, baby. You were right on time."

"I need to get it together. I'm sure I'm going to hear my husband's mouth about staying out all night again, but I don't care. How dare he try and be concerned, when for the last couple of months he couldn't care less."

"Well, at least eat some breakfast. I'll whip up an omelet real quick, so at least you can deal with him on a full stomach," he joked.

"Okay. But he's really going to lose it."

"Want me to come with you?"

Haze must be trying to get me killed. "Now how would that look?"

"It was just an idea. But if you need me, call me."

When we were done eating, I took a shower, got dressed and was ready to leave.

"Remember, call me if you need to."

We stood in front of his door. I really didn't want to go, but I needed to get some rest. If I stayed, Haze and I would've spent all of our time in the bed making love. We kissed one last time, and then I left.

I tried to rehearse what I would say when I got home and walked through the door. I went back and forth with various excuses as to why I didn't make it home. But then I realized that I would've been feeding into his whole "control" thing. *Why should I have to explain where I was? Maybe I could tell him I got a flat.* I chuckled.

It really didn't matter, because Roger was waiting for me outside on the porch when I pulled up. I put the car in park. Normally I would've been full of anxiety, and his firm stance would've intimidated me. But for some strange reason, I was good. I wasn't scared as I got out of the car. I looked at my cell phone to make sure it was on, in case I had to dial 911.

"No missed calls. I wonder what those girls are doing."

Roger didn't take his eyes off of me.

I closed the car door and proceeded to walk up to the front door. I met his gaze. I believe that was the first time I looked him square in his eyes in a long time. He had so much control over my emotions, it was ridiculous. I laughed inside because he had no idea that for the last week or so I'd been spending time with other men, getting loved by complete strangers and loving every minute of it.

Roger didn't like making scenes, so I knew he wouldn't start barking until I was closer to him. When I was about ten yards away from him, I noticed his facial expression change from stern and adamant to skeptical and curious.

"What the hell is wrong with you?"

"Nothing," I calmly responded. "Why do you ask?"

"You come in here smiling after being out all night. I told you before when you pulled this stunt that I wasn't going to tolerate this."

"Roger, I'm grown, and if I want to stay a night, two nights, or however many nights at a friend's house, that's exactly what I'm going to do."

"You think your friends can take care of you?

How about I put your spoiled, unappreciative ass out of my house? What friend would you stay with then?"

"You're not going to do a damn thing. This house is mine just as much as it is yours. Now, you can back up, or I can call the police and they can back you up. What's it going to be, Roger?"

"Keep pushing me, Valen. You'll be sorry."

"Whatever." I walked in the house and closed the door behind me.

It was amazing how a little attention from another man or other men made me see things differently. My confidence level was off the charts. I felt my self-esteem rising.

I thumbed through the mail and saw a check from the escort agency. Along with a check, there was a note from Penelope stating that she gave the crazy dude his money back but paid me for the date anyhow. She apologized and hoped that that one bad date didn't discourage me from going on others.

"You don't have to worry about that," I said to myself. I went to my bedroom and called her to let her know that I got the check and that I was ready for my next date.

Chapter 32

Lyda

When I got home, Boyfriend was on the couch talking on the phone and watching a porno flick on the television.

I nearly drop-kicked his ass. "Aw, hell nah. You mean to tell me that it was you all this time running up my bills?"

"Lyda, when you asked me for the money, I gave it to you, so what's the big deal?"

"The big deal is that when I mentioned it to you, you didn't tell me it was you. You let me blame Anthony all the while. And who are you talking to?" I was hot beyond belief. How could I have been so stupid? I snatched the phone from him.

"I gave you extra money so you can use that to pay for this movie."

"Hello? Who is this?" Two voices on the other line told me that it was some type of 900 number chat line.

"Did he tell you that he has an STD and that's why he has to get his thrills on phone lines like this? That's right, his dick is kind of corroded." I slammed down the phone.

"Are you crazy? Don't tell them that."

"Boyfriend, look, I'm on some different shit now. So I'll tell you what I'm going to do. I'm going to go in my room and close the door, I will count to twenty and come back out and you bes' be gone!"

I went into my bedroom and paced the floor.

Out of all the dudes that I'd dealt with, I gave that asshole the benefit of the doubt. It was the dick. I knew this now because even though Charletta just sexed the shit out me, when I thought of his, my pussy lips applauded it.

Twenty seconds later I came out of my room and that fool was gone. "Good riddance, you simple bastard."

I guess I owed Anthony an apology. All this time I thought it was him trying to play me out. Damn, I felt like shit. Now I had to reach out to him and tell him that I was wrong. *Oh well, everybody has to eat crow some time or another.*

When I called Anthony he laughed at me, which kind of pissed me off. But if that was all he was going to do, then I was cool with that.

"So do you accept my apology?"

"Yeah, I do accept your apology. Do you accept mine when I say that I'm sorry I came at you like that? I mean, you were hitting below the belt by accusing me of not being able to keep it up."

"I know I was. I guess I was being selfish."

"You think? Lyda, did you get yourself checked out?"

"Yes, I did. I thought I told you that."

"Well, I just want to make sure because you know . . ."

"No, I don't know, what?"

"You can make it up to me by letting me come over and give it to you on the real."

I thought about it for a minute. That one time where he did hold out and entertained me for a bit was good. But the dick I just had was good as hell too. And while that was the case, ain't nothing like the real thing. "Okay. What time are you coming by?"

Anthony was at the house in less than an hour. He brought me flowers and a caramel apple.

I didn't eat that kind of stuff, but I took it anyway. I figured I'd give it to Charletta's kids the next time I saw them.

"Are you hungry? If so, we can order something in because I didn't cook."

"No, not for food anyway."

"So what are you saying?" I was trying to get him to talk dirty to me. Charletta drained me, and I needed a little help getting excited.

"I'm saying that I want some ass, some of that ass." He smacked it.

"Then come and get it. Stop thinking that I have to give it to you each time. You need to be a bit more aggressive, that shit turns me on."

Anthony and I got it a couple rounds of rough, exciting sex. He did it this time. He hooked a sistah up for real. I'm talking fifteen, twenty-minute stints of sex. I was like, *Damn!* My coochie held up, everything was everything, and everybody was happy.

Afterwards, we were hungry, so we decided to order some pizza. But before we did that, I called Charletta to see if she was hungry.

"No, but thank you anyway. So did you have a nice time?"

"Did I? Charletta, I had no idea you rolled like that."

"Like what? I'm just doing me. Can't trust or depend on anyone to make sure I'm getting mine, so hey, I have to make sure I'm straight."

"I completely understand. No pizza for you?"

"Nope. None for me."

"Well, have a good night, and I'll see you tomorrow. I have a little treat for the kids and maybe for you too."

"Okay, we'll be waiting."

The pizza came, and Anthony and I had a deep conversation while we ate.

"Lyda, I know you sleep with other men. Why?"

"Anthony, it's just like that. I've always had more than one man because I felt like not one satisfied me enough to settle down."

"Did you give them an honest chance?"

"Everyone has a honest chance. The first time we sleep together, you have to lay that shit down ungodly so that I won't desire another man. Why is it that men think that women don't have their sexuality in check and know what they want? We're human too and don't have to settle for some half-ass dick."

"You're not fair because you thought I was cheating you of the dick when in fact I was having an issue with you. And it wasn't until you kept kicking my back in that I just came right out and told you. Ordinarily, I would've used a different approach, but you backed me into a corner; I felt like you needed to know that you weren't perfect either."

"I know, and I apologize again for that."

"It's cool, but I'm just saying there are good men out there."

"When you find him, can you slide him my phone number please?"

"You're a trip."

"Yeah, I know."

The telephone rang. It was Boyfriend. My first thought was to put Anthony on the phone, but then I thought, *Nah, I could handle this call myself.* "What do you want?"

"So it's like that now?"

"Yeah, just like that. You're a liar, and I can't deal with liars."

" 'Liar'? I'm the liar. Okay, well who's the bigger liar, you or me?"

I knew where he was going, but I wasn't in a position to discuss it at that very moment. I moved into another room so that Anthony couldn't hear me. "Whatever. You just know that you fucked up our little arrangement. Just because I let you come in and chill didn't give you the right to disrespect me like that. Fuck that! I was accusing somebody else for some shit *you* did."

"I'm not worried about that, Lyda. All I want to know is what's up with us? You pulling out or what?"

"I can't discuss this right now. I'll call you tomorrow."

"That's right, because you have company. Yup, I

stayed around and watched your friend come over."

"It's like that sometimes, you know."

"Sure do. Call me tomorrow, Lyda." He hung up the phone in my ear.

I couldn't care less if he decided not to see me any more. I mean, yeah we'd been dealing for a while and he did my body good, but it was taking too much effort and just wasn't worth it any more.

Chapter 33

Jalisa

Even though I knew deep down inside that there was something going on with Quinton, seeing it was worse. I mean, if he was going to cheat, why would he cheat with a little girl? Was this his way of making me feel less than a woman? Was he trying to make me jealous? I could see if he cheated with someone who had more than I did, was prettier, and offered him more than I could. But the way I saw it, a man couldn't ask for anything more than a dedicated wife. She may not have come into the relationship with riches, but if she loved him unconditionally and accepted him with all his faults, then he had a good woman.

I accepted Quinton in the beginning, but when he started blatantly ignoring me and sending me off to get loved by someone else, I was like, *bump that*. That mess was for the birds. Now look at me, I was doing exactly what he said to do, right in the house. No, right in *his* bed.

Darrell sat at the table while I went upstairs and changed the sheets. I knew Quinton wouldn't be coming home because he thought he would have to hear my mouth. In fact, this evening couldn't have worked out better, because now Darrell and I would be able to spend some quality time together.

I called out to him from the top of the stairs. "Darrell."

"What up?"

"Are you coming up here?"

"Where? In your bedroom?"

I nodded yes.

"Hell no. I'm down for whatever, but not that mess. If you want some of this dick, you better bring that ass down here. We can make it happen in the living room, the kitchen, or even in the laundry room on the washer while it's on the spin cycle, but I'm not doing you in your husband's bed."

I cracked up. "Chicken!"

"I'll be that; you heard what I said."

So we did just that. I washed a load, and Darrell and I had sex the entire time the washer was going. The vibration was out of this world as both of us came back to back several times.

He left shortly after, and I took a shower and crawled into bed with my nice, clean sheets.

Around 4:00 a.m., I heard keys jingling in the door. Quinton was home. I was hoping he would sleep on the couch, but I had a feeling he was going to come upstairs and get in the bed. I wasn't bothered by that, I just didn't want any drama. I was tired and wanted to go to sleep.

When I heard him coming up the stairs, I pretended to be in a deep sleep. I had one eye cracked just enough to see what he was doing.

He came into the bedroom, turned on the lights, and tried to look in my face without getting too close, to see if I was awake. He grabbed a pillow and left the room.

The next morning when I woke up and went downstairs, Quinton was asleep on the couch. I went into the kitchen, put on some coffee, turned on the television and the radio and sat down. I knew that would get him up.

"You don't see me sleeping, Jalisa?"

"Yes, I saw you sleeping on the couch."

"So why are you being so rude and turning everything on?"

"You can go upstairs in the bed; I'm up for the day."

When he did that, I called Lyda and Valen. We'd gone a good day or two without talking to each other. Under normal circumstances, that wouldn't happen, but we were all trying to get our groove on, I guess.

"Well, let me tell you, I had some mess go down with Quinton."

"What? Wait, don't tell me, he has a blow up doll just like Roger." Valen laughed.

"No, girl. I went to the restaurant to eat last night, and the hostess was giving me mad attitude. I hadn't seen her there when we were there, so I assumed she was new. But Darrell told me that she was the manager that he was training all along."

"So why was she giving you attitude?" Lyda asked.

"When she gave it to me one time too many, I asked to see the real manager, Quinton. Girl, when he came out, he was all caressing her on the arm and stuff. I told him how she treated me even after I told her who I was, and he took her side. Told me that I must love drama to come down to his restaurant and start trouble."

"Oh, really?" Lyda said.

"I don't understand. What reason would she have to give you attitude?"

"Hold on, I'm getting to that. So after Quinton and I had words, she started running off at the mouth. Luckily, the restaurant was empty because she was getting real 'street' with hers, so much so that Quinton had to drag her off into the kitchen."

Lyda sighed. "Ummm, that's interesting."

"Anyhow, at the same time Darrell came into the restaurant and saw me sitting down. He came over to me, and we talked for a few minutes. He asked me what happened and when I told him, he didn't seem the least bit surprised. He went on to say that she was the night manager and that she and Quinton had been fooling around ever since she began training."

Click.

"Hello?"

"I'm still here. Lyda must've gotten disconnected. Go ahead. We'll fill her in at a later date."

"I got myself up and went into the kitchen after them. When I got in there, I saw them all hugged up in each other's arms."

"No way, Jalisa."

"Yes way, girl. I lost it. I grabbed her funky butt and tried to snap her neck. I spat in both of their faces. Darrell came behind me and was buggin'. He laughed a little and when I was done with those fools, I told him to come with me. Let me tell you what that fool did. He quit his job and told Quinton that he couldn't work for him as long as he was fucking me." I busted out laughing, and so did Valen.

"Oh my gosh! No, he didn't. Girl, I don't know what I would've done. It's one thing to suspect, but to actually see it is a completely different story."

"Valen, I was done the first time I let Steven do it to me. It was inevitable that he or I be found out. It just so happened that he was careless and got caught first."

"You right, our game is definitely tighter than theirs."

"So you and Darrell went where? Back to your house?"

"Yup. I invited him upstairs, but he wouldn't come. Instead he fucked me on the washer while I did a load of sheets. Which reminds me, do you remember the dude who hit the lottery for a little bit of money and gave some to Lyda? Well, he and I had a little interlude too. He wasn't as scared as Darrell. He tore this ass up right in Quinton's bed."

"What, girl! You are so crazy."

"Sure am. That's just how far Quinton has pushed me."

Chapter 34

Valen

"I'm not mad at you. I had a few things going on too. You know I did that escort thing, right?"

"Yeah. I would've never imagined."

"Well, things happen let me finish, girl so the first night went okay. I had a date with Haze. By the way, he's a really nice guy. The thugged-out thing could be me for a minute. We had a really nice time together.

"My next date was just plain crazy. I walked out before we even ordered because he was tripping. He started yelling at me, saying stuff like my husband didn't know where I was, and all this mess. I was scared."

"You never know the type of people you run into with those jobs, Valen you better be careful."

"I know. So when I walked out on him I saw the AAA man who fixed my tire on Route 18. He was towing a car that was parked in front of the car garage where I parked my car. I was so shaken up from 'crazy man' that I didn't want to go right home. I invited him out for coffee. One thing led to another, and the next thing I knew, we were at the Holiday Inn having sex."

"You had sex with him? What is his name anyway?"

"Reid. I don't know his last name. I have his card somewhere. Anyway, I ended up staying the night with him. When I came home Roger and I had it out."

"I bet you did."

"Yeah, well I stayed out again last night when I spent the night with Haze."

"Oh, you just cutting up, I see."

"And when I came home Roger was waiting outside for me. He started with his mess, but I shut him down real quick. I told him I was a grown woman. I'll do what I want."

"Wow! It's amazing what they've turned us into. These men these days should be careful how they treat their women."

"You are so right. I'm about to get me some sleep. Catch up with me later."

"Cool. I guess Lyda wasn't interested in hearing what we had going on; she didn't call back."

"Guess not. She's probably getting some."

When I got off the phone, I fell back onto my pillow. I thought about Reid. He was truly a good guy, but Haze had me thinking that I could sneak off to his place when I wanted some time to myself. No one would know where I was. He didn't live in my neck of the woods, so his place was the perfect spot.

Then it hit me, the last time we had sex, he didn't use a condom. I didn't remember wiping of his juices, which means that he came inside of me. "Damn it! "That was careless."

I wrote down the date on a piece of paper. If I didn't get my period when it was expected, in about a week or so, then I would need to get a pregnancy test along with a full blood work up. Exhausted, I curled up in my bed and went to sleep.

Chapter 35

Lyda

"I need to talk to you?"

"About what?" Boyfriend asked.

"I think you know. When can you come over?"

"I'll be there in a little while."

See, these dudes thought we don't get hip to their games. He knew coming in that I had other men that I dated, but he never mentioned that he was seeing someone else or even thought about seeing someone else. That wasn't something that I could deal with. I understood his situation and that was it. Nothing else was discussed, and I feel like he lied to me by not telling me if his feelings changed, if the arrangement we had wasn't working any more or whatever.

While I waited for him to come over, I called Charletta to see if now was a good time to give her the candy apple for the kids.

"I normally don't let them eat that kind of stuff, but since it's from you, I'll make an exception."

Charletta cut it up into equal pieces and split it amongst the two of them. The kids were excited. They went to watch television, and Charletta and I talked in the kitchen.

"Can I offer you a glass of wine?"

"Yes, I could really use one right about now."

"What's wrong?"

"Nothing. I think I'm just tired from yesterday, you really showed me something." Granted we'd shared a very intimate moment, I didn't want to burden Charletta with my current problem.

"I hope I didn't push too hard. I really wanted you. And I know you were shocked, but I don't exactly go around broadcasting my sexuality."

"What is your sexuality? Are you gay or bisexual?"

"I don't characterize it. I like what I like, and if it's a woman on this day and a man on that day, then that's what it is. Pleasure is pleasure and shouldn't have to come from one source."

"Yes, you're right, Charletta." That made perfect sense to me. Look at what I'd been doing for years, sleeping with two and three men at a time. And just when I thought I didn't care what they did when they weren't with me, I hear something and can't deal.

I heard a car door close. I went to look out the window to see Boyfriend walking up.

"Listen, don't pour this out. I'll be back in a little while. I just have to take care of something." I gave Charletta a kiss on the cheek and left out.

I met Boyfriend at my front door, and we went in. I asked him, "Is there something that you want to tell me?"

"No, not really. Should there be?"

I had a feeling he knew what I was talking about, but I wanted him to come out and say it.

"What are you talking about, Lyda?"

"Are you fucking somebody else?"

He laughed in my face. And I don't mean a chuckle, I mean a full, gut-wrenching, eye-tearing laugh. I wished I could've taken that question back.

"Lyda, you're not serious. After all we've talked about and the understanding we had, you have the nerve to ask me if I have someone else. Who's the one with not one, but two and three sexual partners at one time? You, not me."

"Please . . . you knew that going into this, though."

"Wait, let me finish. Yes, I knew this, but we also agreed that you wouldn't flaunt your friends in my face, right?"

"Yes, what's your point? And who did I flaunt in your face?"

"The day that dude was coming out of your house when I pulled up, who was that?"

"That was Anthony, we're just friends." I didn't think that was a lie, because at the time, I'd only slept with him once maybe twice; he wasn't a steady partner.

"A friend. Lyda, I'm not stupid. I also know that you met up with some other dude who came over here and laid down the pipe as well, the married one, I'm sure you know who I'm talking about."

"Quincy?"

"I guess so. I didn't get his name when he was coming out. I just walked past him, looked at his finger and saw that he was married."

"I know Quincy from back in the day. We're old friends."

"Did he fuck you when he was here?"

"What?"

"You heard me, did you fuck him?"

"Yes, I did. But again, you knew I had friends who I would hook up when we decided to hook up."

"I know, Lyda, but it doesn't seem to ever end with you. You keep getting more and more friends, and when I get another one, you want to trip. Come on now, you know that's not right."

"All I'm saying is, why didn't you tell me? Why did I have to hear about it in the streets?"

"It's like that sometimes. If you were completely honest with me, I would've been completely honest with you. So now the question is, what are we going to do about this little problem we have?"

"I think you need to leave that girl alone."

"Yeah? Then I think you need to leave that girl next door alone. Um hum, didn't think I knew about that either, right?"

I was cold busted. "Look okay, maybe I should've told you that I broadened my horizons, but I really didn't think you would care. I mean, we have an open relationship, so I didn't think it was a big deal."

"Well, it was, but it isn't any longer. I have to go to now. I have to open up the restaurant."

"Wait." He walked right out my door.

"Quinton, please wait." I followed him outside and watched him as he drove off.

Charletta stood in her doorway. She lifted my wineglass and invited me in.

Chapter 36

Jalisa

Stephen, Darrell, and I made a date to meet at my office. Since we'd had a threesome and everyone was okay with how it went down, we decided that it could be something that we could engage in once in a while. I also wanted to address the unprotected sex that we had. I'd slipped up and had unprotected sex with Terry too, and since then I'd been having this tingly feeling in my vagina that I needed to go and get checked out.

I asked Stephen, "So when we're not all together, do you have a problem with me hooking up with Darrell?"

"No, not at all; in fact, I encourage it. And if you guys ever feel like you want to be exclusive, don't worry about me. I'll be okay." He and Darrell gave each other a high-five.

"We did something really risky by not having protected sex."

"I agree, and that's something we need to be very aware of. I mean, I have my wife, and I'm sure Darrell has his people that he sees. So if we could all be careful, I think that we can have a good time and feel confident that we're all in good hands."

"I do have one or two people I hook up with, but I used protection with them. So you're cool as far as I'm concerned. What about you? Have you had sex with anyone other than your husband that we should know about?"

"Well, my husband and I don't have sex. Again, that's why I do what I do, but yes, there was one other person who I had sex with unprotected. I don't think we have anything to worry about because he's just not that type of guy, but I will get the appropriate tests done and show you the negative results."

I laughed it off, but I do recall Terry not taking a shower after we were together. I wondered if he did that with all of the people he slept with. I needed to get checked out quick just to be safe.

"That's a good idea, Jalisa. We'll get tested too, and this way everyone will be at ease."

That afternoon, I went to Planned Parenthood in Shrewsbury to get tested. The tingly feeling I had turned into an itch, and little bumps formed at the top of my vagina. Normally I wouldn't be concerned, but since my sexual lifestyle had changed, I was.

They tested me for AIDS and other sexually transmitted diseases. It took 48 hours to get the results, so all I could do was wait. I gave them my cell phone number to contact me instead of the house phone because Quinton didn't need to know anything.

In the meantime, I called Lisette. She'd been holding it down in California for me. I wanted to go out to see her, but with everything that was going on, I hadn't had the time to sit down and plan a trip. Everything was going great out there. She had picked up a few clients and advised me that she would be e-mailing me their contact information soon. I really appreciated her and would've really liked to go and spend some time.

Two days later, I got the call from Planned Parenthood. I was diagnosed with genital herpes. There was no cure for it, just treatment. They wanted to see everyone I had sexual contact with so that they could be tested. I learned that most people didn't even know that they had the virus, herpes could be dormant for weeks, months, and sometimes years. So, in theory, I could've gotten it from Quinton, who could've gotten it from that girl he'd been messing around with and God knows who else.

My heart plummeted. How could I have been so careless to not protect myself? I knew one thing for sure, I didn't have this feeling after I slept with Stephen, or after the threesome with Stephen and Darrell. It was after I slept with Terry that I began to get that tingly feeling and with the way he left out of here without washing, I bet I got that mess from him

They prescribed Zovirax pills and cream for my treatment. I was so embarrassed with my condition that I went to a different pharmacy, rather than my normal pharmacy, because not only did I not want them in my business, but the last thing I needed was for them to mention something to Quinton.

My first thought was to call Terry and give him a piece of my mind, but then I thought about it. I would look stupid asking him if he had herpes when I was the one diagnosed with it. And you know how men are, if they do have it, they won't admit it. They'd go and get tested, get the positive results, and swear that the woman gave it to them. I decided not to call him on that. This was my problem, and I would deal with it myself. I had to tell my girls, though.

Chapter 37

Valen

When I woke up, I wanted to talk to Haze. I got a shower, got dressed, and headed out without saying a word to Roger. He was in his office working. I didn't even look at him on the way out, but I could feel his eyes on me.

While I was in the car, I called Haze. "Hey there. Feel like some company?"

"Baby, I always feel like some you." Haze knew how to lay it on thick.

I thought about the possibility of being pregnant. Would I be a good mother? Would I be able to live with the fact that I cheated and bore another man's child? I feel like Roger pushed me to this point. Something like this was bound to happen because while I was out there trying to validate my womanhood, I lost sight of the importance of protecting myself. I shook my head in disbelief that I had put myself in this predicament.

When I got to Haze's apartment, the door was already open.

"Hello," I said as I knocked and walked in.

"In here," he yelled.

He was in the kitchen writing rhymes. He looked handsome with all his jewelry and his thugged-out gear. "Hey, baby, how you doing?" He got up and kissed me on the lips.

I melted inside. "I'm good. I just wanted to come and see you."

"That's what's good, baby. You want a beer or something?"

"Oh no. I think I've had enough to last me a while, a long while. But there is something I want to talk to you about."

"Okay . . . I'm listening." He put his pen down and gave me his undivided attention.

"The other day, the last time we had sex, did we use protection?" I wanted him to tell me because I was too buzzed to remember and maybe he did.

"No." He shook his head. "No, Valen, we didn't, and I thought about that after the fact and wondered if you were upset about it. But don't worry, let me show you something." He got up and went into his bedroom.

He returned with a paper from a doctor's office. "I get tested yearly for everything. Now this is two months old, but I have no problems taking you with me and getting tested again, if that would make you feel better."

I took the piece of paper and looked over it then handed it back to him. "I appreciate your honesty, and if I feel something different going on down there, I'll let you know. But I'm really more concerned with getting pregnant."

Haze had a blank stare on his face. He picked up the pen and began to tap it on the counter top.

I didn't know if he was about to go off or what, so I just waited for his response.

"If you get pregnant, then I'll be a daddy. I'll stand by you against your husband, and we'd deal with it."

"Okay." Part of me was relieved, but then the other part of me was scared. *Roger would die if I got pregnant. Would he wonder if he was the father?* We'd stopped having sex just about two weeks ago, so I didn't think he would suspect anything.

A week later, I took a pregnancy test, which came out positive.

Haze was with me when I cried on the floor of his bathroom. He held me close and reaffirmed his position.

"We will get through this; you won't be alone."

Though his words were kind, I didn't feel any better. I was pregnant by him and had to tell Roger at some point. I got myself together and made my way home.

"If you think this is funny, Valen, then you're really crazy. All you've done for the last week or two was run the streets like you don't have a home."

" 'A home'? You call this a home? All you've done was beat me down with your hateful words and foul treatment and made it so that I didn't want to be here. Roger you had to know that eventually I would get fed up. How much of that treatment do you think a person can take?"

"All I ever tried to do was give you a good life, and all I asked for in return was a little respect."

"Roger, respect is a two-way street. All you ever tried to do was control me, and when you finally realized that you couldn't, you demeaned me instead."

"Valen," he said, softening his voice, "I know I haven't been the perfect husband. I've had time to understand how my actions and my words may have affected you. I will make a conscious effort to be more aware of your feelings and your needs."

"A blow up doll, Roger? Come on. How do you ever expect me to bounce back from that? Just because I'm pregnant doesn't mean that you can change into this loving and caring person. A baby needs parents who can love them unconditionally and accept them for who they are; you just aren't that type of person. It's just too late, Roger."

Chapter 38

Lyda

Quinton was right. He hit the nail on the head when he said that I broke our arrangement. When he and I first hooked up, it was supposed to be only one time. We had no idea that we would mesh the way we did. Initially, I was against it, but he was so persistent. All he did was complain about how Jalisa didn't satisfy him. I felt bad.

Because I had my men that I spent time with, I figured if I broke him off a little here and there, he would be satisfied. Well turned out, I was the one who couldn't get enough.

When I say that Quinton wasn't the brightest crayon in the box, I meant that from the standpoint that he cut Jalisa off like that. He didn't wean himself off of her. The minute I gave him the panties, Jalisa got no more dick. She was done. Naturally any woman would suspect their man of cheating if one day they're all lovey-dovey and the next they're cold as ice. I told him though, "Give her a little. All she needs is enough to make her feel that she's still number one in your heart. But no, he got hooked on me, I got hooked on him, and that was that.

So what he did was try his hardest not to be around Jalisa and me at the same time, and for the most part, he succeeded. It was when I would call and ask to speak to her that he would hear my voice and want to come holla. I would try to help him out and start little tiffs between either him and Jalisa, or him and me. I was the one who created the notion that we didn't get along when the truth was, that very same night, he would be in my bed fucking the shit out of me only an hour after Jalisa called me and complained about his coldness.

Now the average person would ask the question, "How could someone do that to somebody they considered to be a true friend?" My answer to that was simple. If you don't look out for you, who will? You have to create your own happiness no matter what, and sometimes people get hurt in the process.

To be honest, Quinton wasn't going to see me any more. He was able to deal with the men I already had in my life, but he couldn't deal with Anthony, Quincy, or Charletta. He didn't want the new competition. He didn't consider those who were already sleeping with me any competition because he was the new kid on the block and probably thought if they were all that, I wouldn't hook up with him.

He was all right for a while, but then he began

to get too needy, showing up at my door, always wanting to wait for me at my house. No, that was too much for me. It was no sweat off of my back, though. Quincy, Charletta, and Anthony were going to keep me busy for a long time to come, and if not then I'd move on to someone else.

Chapter 39

Jalisa

"Valen, get Lyda on the three-way."

Once she got Lyda on the line, I began my story. "I have vaginal herpes."

"What?" Valen said.

"That's some nasty shit. How? And from who?"

"Well, that's a stupid question. It can only be transmitted sexually, and if I had to say anyone, I would say Terry."

"Terry-that-gave-me-the-money Terry?" Lyda asked.

"Yes, that Terry."

"Well, it's a good thing I didn't sleep with him."

"Girl, I am so upset."

"Jalisa, how would you know? I mean, we've all made mistakes and slept with people unprotected, and sometimes there are consequences for that."

Lyda asked me, "Jalisa, did you sleep with Quinton after you slept with Terry?"

"No. You know that why would you ask such a question?"

"Well, because if you did, then nine times out of ten you gave it to him. All I'm saying is that I know you guys are having problems, but you owe it to him to tell him if you got the 'cooties.' "

"Lyda, this is not the time for your jokes. This is a very serious matter, so please, if you can't just listen without making funnies, then hang up."

"Relax, Valen. I was just saying—"

"And so was I." Valen snapped at Lyda. "Speaking of unprotected sex, I'm pregnant."

"Oh lawd!" Lyda sang.

"What, Valen! By who?"

Man, I was glad I wasn't the only one dropping bombs.

"Haze. We had unprotected sex the last time we slept together; I don't know how I got so careless."

"Did you tell Roger?" I asked.

"Yes. And you would not believe what his response was."

Lyda blurted out, "Whose was it."

"No. This fool actually thought he could convince me that he's had a lot of time to think about how he'd been treating me and that he was sorry. I simply told him it was too late."

"He didn't accuse you of sleeping around?" Lyda asked. "I'm shocked."

"Why would you be shocked? I don't sleep around, *you* do, bye Lyda." Valen cut her off, leaving just the two of us on the phone.

"So are you going to keep the baby?"

"Yes. I can't have an abortion."

"Wow! Valen, you know I'm here for you."

"Yes, Jalisa, and thank you so much for that. What about you? I would imagine that your lifestyle has to change."

"I am so upset about this, but yes, I will have to have protected sex so that I don't pass the virus to anyone else. And when I have outbreaks, I can't have sex at all."

"How often will you get those?"

"I could get them once a month or once a year. If I get stressed out, I can get one, if I get a bad period, I can get one, or a bad cold could bring it on too."

"Well, it looks like we really need each other now, Jalisa. Maybe Lyda will stop being so self-centered and realize that as well."

"Maybe. Maybe not.